ABOUT THE AUTHOR

Jennifer Manson is a writer and business woman. She lives in Christchurch, New Zealand, with her husband, two teenage children and two cats. She is the author of "The Moment of Change" and "The Old Occidental Writers' Hotel" and also writes for The Press newspaper's "at home" supplement.

Tasha Stuart interviews . . .

Jennifer Manson

ACKNOWLEDGEMENTS

To my writing buddy and greatest supporter, poet Kerrin P. Sharpe;

To my inspiring friend and business associate, Wendy Davie at Totally Organised, www.totallyorganised.co.nz;

To my readers: Vicki Slade, Stephanie Royds and Caryn Hardy;

To my daughter, Alex, my son, Jono, and my wonderful husband, Paul;

To the inspiring Stuart Fleming, in whose honour Tasha was named;

To Dan Poynter, whose timely, astute and generous advice lead to my getting into print so soon;

To Richard Koch, author of "The 80/20 Principle," for the hugely attractive concept of combining extreme ambition with a relaxed and confident manner;

To P!nk, for reminding intelligent women how to have fun;

And to Malcolm Gladwell, for being a genius - so many of my ideas about life are, in fact, his;

Thank you.

All characters in this book, with the exception of
'Organising Guru', Wendy, are fictitious
and any resemblance to real persons,
living or dead, is purely coincidental.

1

Bernard was waiting for me at the café. He filled the doorway like a dark shadow.

"How's my gorgeous sister-in-law?" He kissed me on the cheek, hand lingering on my waist.

"Good. You?"

I pulled up the grill over the front door and window and unlocked the door, letting him in before me. I never like to let Bernard get between me and the exit. He lounged against the counter while I began my morning routine. I make the sandwiches and put the pies in the warmer before Scott arrives to start on his more sophisticated dishes. I prayed Scott would be early this morning.

I kept losing concentration as Bernard regaled me with his drunken exploits from the weekend. As I passed to give the tables another wipe over I could have sworn I felt an arm brush my breast. When I turned to object, however, he was finishing a natural looking yawn and stretch, eyes on the ceiling.

"Not going to be late for work are you?"

"No appointments 'till 10. Man of leisure 'till then. Immigrant wanting a cleaning business, piece of piss – easy to use the language barrier to my advantage, don't have to be as careful what I say, so should be an easy $3,000 commission. That'll keep the wolves from the door for the day." He reached into the warmer, pulled out a sausage roll and sagged onto a chair, dropping crumbs onto the freshly cleaned table. "So if you need any more money, I'll be fine to increase your loan." His words were muffled in his full mouth.

I run a little café near Cathedral Square in Christchurch, New Zealand, between the library and the tourist shops. To be honest it's not that successful, though I'm never sure why not. We have lots of customers, cheerful staff. Maybe it's that I don't like putting my prices up, even when the rent increases. The loan Bernard was talking about was from buying new tables and chairs the year before last.

I don't really like feeling under financial pressure all the time; at the same time there's a feeling of familiarity that has a kind of back-handed comfort. Until Bernard turns up, that is.

I wriggled uncomfortably. "Actually I was trying to think how I can repay what I already owe you. Maybe it's time to call it a day with the café. Maybe I'll try something new . . . How much is the loan now?"

He pulled out his Blackberry with a sour expression. "$11,000, all up."

"But that's more than it was to begin with!"

"Yeah, well you were late with a few payments, you know that."

I felt sick. I had tried to talk to Steven about Bernard, but we hadn't fully discussed the details of my borrowing from him, and the inappropriate brushes were never quite enough to complain about. "He's a bit of a dick, but he's got a good heart," was all Steven said. I had the feeling he didn't want to know any more.

I wished I'd insisted and just increased the mortgage like I wanted to, but Steven didn't want to put the house at risk.

"I could always sell the business for you," Bernard continued. "We'd have to fake the numbers a bit, find an unsuspecting idealist, but those are ten a penny . . . I've got an agency agreement in the car."

I scratched my head and screwed up my eyes. "No, I'm not sure yet. I'll let you know."

Scott appeared in the doorway and Bernard stood up and oozed out the door.

"What was the old lech doing here?"

"Same as usual."

"It's time we got you a panic button installed. Da da da la da da dah! Scott to the rescue!" His cheerful face fell as mine crumpled into tears; he put an arm awkwardly around me. "Come on, Boss, you know this comforting stuff isn't in my job description." But this time I just couldn't hitch up my smile.

TASHA STUART INTERVIEWS . . .

2

I sat back into my chair, wine glass in hand and sighed out my frustration.

"I blew it again. Fifteen fabulously interesting people in the room and I just talk about me, me, me. I don't think I closed my mouth for ten minutes the whole evening."

"You're too hard on yourself. You were quiet while the speaker was talking." Wendy kept her face serious for a few moments, then burst out laughing when I gave her my hard stare.

"Oh . . . drink your wine." I gave my head a little shake, like a duck recovering poise after a fight.

Wendy smirked again and leaned her head on the chair back. "Just enjoy yourself, lose the analysis. It was a great night."

This was my second visit to the National Speakers' Association. Wendy's a great speaker but I'm not a natural. One-on-one I'm fluent, engaging, but put me in front of a group of people and I only recover consciousness once I have been lead by the hand back to my seat.

She's much more relaxed than me in lots of ways. Wendy Rob-Williams, the vibrant founder of Outrageously Organised, New Zealand's original Professional Organising company – she does what she likes, dresses how she likes and says what she likes. Attempting to emulate her extreme ambition and relaxed and confident manner has lead me into more terrifying situations than I can remember – largely because of that thing of becoming an amnesiac through fear.

Tonight, though, I hadn't completely embarrassed myself, just missed the opportunity to learn from the fascinating people I talked to. Half a scintillating sentence and I am off on some rapid, thought-associated leap into a far off subject, never to return to the original idea.

Finally the barman pulled down the grill on the bar and turned off the lights. We hugged at the door as we headed for opposite car parks. Wendy's orange sequined scarf caught in my hair, distracting us both from my parting monologue. Before I could recover to continue she patted my arm. "Go easy on yourself. We all love you. I'll call you tomorrow."

Back home, next to my adorable snoring husband, I couldn't sleep. "There must be some way I can learn to shut up and listen," I thought as I stared at the dim shadows on the ceiling, the sceptical voice inside my head telling me that that was just as likely as having a business which actually worked. All the same, I kept turning the idea over and over in my mind.

I woke the next morning with two words repeating like a mantra: professional interviewer, professional interviewer.

"What the hell is that?" I wondered.

3

That morning, once the setup was done and Scott was underway in the kitchen, I sat down at a table with a pen in my hand. "Throw me one of those notebooks, would you? In the drawer by the till."

The book came flying across the room. Scott doesn't talk much while he's working, the first customers had come and gone and there was no-one in – the rush would start around ten.

"What do I want?" I wrote.

Freedom

Laughter

Friends

To be brave

A bigger house

A dog

Flexible work

Financial success

Here I slumped and the list petered out. How was this ever going to be possible? If I hadn't done it by now . . .

I stared over at Scott. I like watching him in the kitchen, he has a wiry agility and sinuous flow that captivates the eye; his short cropped hair and streamlined cycling shorts add to the sense of sculpture in motion.

"Scott . . ?" I said vaguely, chewing my pen.

"Yah?"

"Can you think of any way we could make this place more successful? Make more money."

It was like someone had wound him up. He sprang upright from the tomato he was slicing and wiped his hands on his apron.

"There's loads we could do," he said eagerly. "For starters, the prices are low but the clientele aren't price sensitive – they're all suits who love the location and the taste. Fifty cents here or there wouldn't make a difference to them, and in some cases it could double your profit on an item. That sign isn't eye-catching enough and we throw too much away."

I sat back and let my arm fall by my side. "Why didn't you mention any of this before?"

He picked up his knife again. "You never asked. And . . ."

"Yes?"

"If it were me I'd get rid of that bloodsucking brother-in-law and refinance the loan."

"How did you . . ?"

"I've got ears and eyes – and an excellent sense of mood. He makes you scared and miserable whenever he comes in. If it were me I'd just kick the bastard out and have done. Restraining order wouldn't go astray, either."

"But who else would lend me the money? I don't . . . I've never . . ."

"Never made any money? I know. But you could, you really could. If it were mine I'd make it pay."

I watched the hypnotic movement of his knife for a minute or two, thinking hard, then shook my head. "Where am I going to get $11,000?"

Scott's knife descended slowly onto the bench top and he raised his eyes to mine. "$11,000? You are making yourself this unhappy for a paltry $11,000? I thought it must be much more! I could lend you that much myself!"

I called Wendy and we met up. "What shall I do? I don't know if I even want the café any more."

"Well, do you or don't you? What do you love about it?"

"Love? Well, I like the customers, and the people I work with are great. But I hate having to be there every day, I hate the juggle when the children are sick and in the holidays. I hate not making money – God, it's not even a business, businesses make money, it's a hobby – the best that can be said is that it keeps me out of the shops."

"And you think you want to keep it, why?"

I stared out the window. I could feel a tear forming. "I just hate the idea of everyone thinking I'm a failure." I looked down and started pulling loose bits of wool from my jumper. My head was aching and I could feel sobs brewing in my back but they wouldn't come. I peeked up at Wendy. She was watching me with interest.

"So, what do you want to do?"

"I don't know!" I wailed.

"Yes you do. What do you want to do?"

"I want to get out. I want to have my time to myself and my thoughts to myself and I want to be happy again. I feel like I haven't been happy for so long."

"So sell it. Sell the business."

"For what? A business broker would look at the books. I don't want anyone else knowing I'm a failure and it wouldn't do any good anyway. They'll say it's not worth anything."

"When you're finished with the drama, let me know, will you? What do you own?"

"What do you mean?"

"In the café – what do you own? You rent the building, but inside."

"Well . . . the stock, food and stuff, the plates and cups and knives. And those bloody chairs and tables."

"And you said Scott had enough to pay off Bastard Bernard. So sell it to him and walk free."

It was like my lungs expanded fully for the first time in years.

"It's just possible. God, what would I do then?"

"I don't know, Babe, but I can't wait to find out."

What would I do then? I asked myself the question and that mantra came back again: professional interviewer. Asking questions and sitting quiet while a fascinating expert talked about what they knew. It would solve that compulsive talking thing. It would be fun. And maybe it would even make a viable business. But where would I start?

Scott was wearing a hangdog expression. He fancies Maria, the part-time waitress, but she's so beautiful she has an automatic brush-off reflex that is charming, and therefore devastating. I complimented his caramel slice to cheer him up and he gave me a weak smile. This was not the time to ask if he'd buy the café. Maybe I'd look at this interviewing idea a little closer before I made a move.

I opened the till and was reminded I hadn't been able to stock a full float this morning. Money. Or lack of it. How did I get here?

When things got quiet in the half hour before lunch I slipped next door to the library. Interviews, but who? Following a vague pull, walking in circles which widened then narrowed, I found myself in the biography section. I looked through the titles: politicians – I'm too ignorant; sports people – ditto; media personalities, actors and film directors – maybe I could do that.

I came back to my point of frustration, people I meet on a day-to-day basis who are passionate about their work or their hobbies or their local causes. I realised I wanted to start closer to home.

I grabbed one of those little pieces of paper they have for you to write shelf references on and pulled the tethered pen to its full extent.

I need:

Recording equipment

Somewhere quiet to record

People willing to be interviewed

A forum to share the interviews once they were done

I sighed and went back to work.

"Scott, you know about recording."

Scott's a musician in his spare time, with occasional gigs to keep him excited about it. He plays bass and guitar and sings a little. I've been to see his band – a little complex for my taste, but they have a core following of frustrated young men.

"A bit, not really."

"I want to get a recorder, you know for recording things." I am quite articulate sometimes, really.

"What sort of thing?"

"Oh, like conversations . . . people talking."

"I'll have a look, let you know."

The next day he came back with comprehensive Internet research, comparisons on size and sound quality and price. We picked one, ordered it and stretched my credit card to the limit. I was getting quite excited until I realised I still had no one to start on.

"Wendy?" I began timidly, calling her at her office. "How do you feel about giving an interview?"

"To who?" She's been on TV, radio, people are fascinated by this Professional Organising thing. She's even done a book tour.

"To me."

There was a short, surprised silence on the end of the phone, then "Sure, when?"

"When are you free?"

4

I was ridiculously nervous. I had lain awake wondering what to ask Wendy. Should it be a 'How-to' interview, with useful content? A biography starting from humble origins in the suburbs? I had settled on how she got started in the organising industry, and we'd see where we went from there.

I had tested the recorder, unimaginative "1, 2, 3s" downloaded onto my computer and played back through the editing software that Scott had installed. He had explained it to the point I could do the simplest things, beyond that my brain was in overload. It looked like a taser. I hoped Wendy wouldn't be frightened. Or even laugh. I didn't think I could take it.

I had another check list:

Be professional

Treat the subject like a star

Ask interesting questions

Shut up and listen

Ask more interesting questions which relate to the answers of the
first interesting questions

Finish with a credit for myself

I ushered Wendy into her chair. "Would you like a glass of water, cup of tea?"

I slopped the water and only just moved the recorder out of the way in time. It took me ten minutes to untangle the lapel mikes and work out which way around to put on the clips. Wendy sat patiently, looking around the room.

"Is that picture new?"

I was too preoccupied to answer.

Finally the thing was ready, the record button pressed once for sound levels ("Say something" "Say what?" "That's fine.") and again to start recording. Almost immediately I stopped it again. "What do you want me to say about you?"

She raised her eyebrows.

I thought wildly. "What about 'Wendy Rob-Williams is the founder of Outrageously Organised, New Zealand's original Professional Organising company. She is here today to talk to us about how she got started in this business.' "

"That sounds fine."

I started the recorder again. "Wendy Rob-Williams is the founder . . . wait . . . Wendy Rob-Williams is the founder . . . Wendy Rob-Williams is . . . . Wendy Rob-Williams . . . shit . . . Wendy . . ." I was hyperventilating. She handed me her glass and I took a gulp of water, choking and spraying it over the coffee table, the $800 voice recorder and my long-suffering subject.

She took a tissue and dried her face. "Let's try that again."

"I think I better write it down."

Three more goes and I got it, then there were a few more stumbles and a pause while I wrote down my first question. "Wendy, tell us how you got started in this business." And then I closed my mouth and a miracle happened. She began to talk, and I shut up and listened.

She was fascinating. I learned things I hadn't known after three years of friendship; interesting things, things I could learn from. The next question followed naturally "did it take a lot of courage to take the plunge?" and she was off again. An hour flew by and I had had the time of my life. Of course, I stumbled over my final credit until she wrote that down for me, too. "Wendy Rob-Williams was interviewed by professional interviewer Tasha Stuart, www.tashastuart.co.nz."

She waved away my thanks, laughing. "I had a great time."

I couldn't wait to get to the editing, but I had the kids to collect from school. Backing the car out of the drive I was certain I was onto something. I felt a new path stretching out in front of me.

TASHA STUART INTERVIEWS . . .

5

"Can't you do it?"

Scott rolled his eyes. "No. Again, no. You have to do it yourself."

"But I just can't. I've never stood up to anyone in my life. And what if Bernard doesn't accept this amount? It's less than he's expecting."

"It's all worked out: the original amount, the agreed interest, the penalties for the late payments. Just give him the letter and the cheque and tell him to go."

"What if he . . . what if he . . ?"

"He's a bastard, but what can he do, really?"

I pondered. There was a nameless dread, but I didn't imagine any clear or specific threat. Did I think Bernard would hit me? No, he was never as direct as that.

"I'm not taking over the café until he's out of it. It has to be done. I'll be standing over there pretending not to listen."

"But . . ."

"Tasha, you can actually do this."

I looked up into Scott's eyes and felt my shoulders pull back. "Okay. You go over there and pretend not to be listening. I'll stand here and tell him he's out."

"Good idea."

The letter was shaking in my hand. I ran my eyes over it again. 'Dear Mr. Wendel, please find enclosed full payment discharging all Ms. T. Stuart's responsibilities under the loan agreement drawn up between you and dated three years ago, a copy of which is attached. Final payment has been calculated according to agreed interest rates and penalties as on the attached sheet. A cheque for $8,746.23 is enclosed. Thank you for your assistance in offering the loan. As the café is now changing ownership, it would be appreciated if you would pay for all food consumed from this point onwards.'

I paced back and forth. Waiting was horrible. I felt my courage slip and hitched it back up again.

Bernard slouched in with a curious expression. I had never summoned him here before. He's taller than Steven, and broader, but has the same dark hair and steel-blue eyes. I avoided his gaze, turning my eyes down to the letter in my hand.

"Good news." My voice was shaking. "I've got the money to repay your loan."

His face darkened, actually darkened, more blood in it than before. "What do you mean?"

I didn't answer. I thought my meaning was clear.

"What do you mean?" he said again, louder.

I handed him the sheaf of papers, which he glanced at and threw onto a table.

"I'm selling the café. I told you. I'm moving on to something else. Actually I've already sold it."

"You said I could sell it!"

"I . . ."

"We had a verbal agreement." He stepped closer to me.

I cast my mind back over the conversations we had had about him brokering a sale for me. They had never actually been conversations, just monologues I hadn't contradicted. He was too close to my face. "No, Bernard, we didn't. Please just read the letter, it's all in there."

"No I bloody won't read the letter. You can't do this. We had an agreement."

His face was purple and very ugly. I stepped backwards and a look of triumph crossed his face as he stepped closer again. My eyes closed. I took a deep shuddering breath and opened my eyes again. I took one small step toward him. "I can do it. I have done it. Now go."

His head pulled back a few millimetres in surprise and that was all it took to give me the advantage. He had begun his retreat. I stepped forward again, picked up the papers and handed them to him. "Go."

He turned, uncertain, and walked to the door. Outside on the pavement he turned again. "I'll be back" he said, with little conviction.

"You come back if you want to, Bernard. You won't find me here."

I stood paralysed, my heart thumping and my breath short.

"Tasha . . ." he held out his hand and took half a step back towards me. "Please. Tasha, this won't affect our friendship, will it?" My mouth dropped open. Friendship? For a terrible moment before Scott closed the door between us, I thought I saw a tear in Bernard's eye.

"Great work!" Scott flipped the closed sign, pulled down the blind and locked the door. "Great work!" He swung me in the air. My hand was over my mouth and I wasn't sure if I was laughing or crying. "Hey!" he said, as tears dropped onto my cheek. "You did it, girl! You'll never be the same again."

I crumpled into a seat. "Bring me tea. Bring me chocolate." I lay my arms on the table, put my head on them and let the sobs shake my body clean.

6

Scott brought the tea and waited while I drank a few sips. I looked up at him, my new freedom breaking out in an impish smile. I was feeling something I didn't quite recognise.

He grinned back. "Ready for the next thing?" He drew the Sale and Purchase papers for the café out of his backpack. I had tried to get him to sign them earlier in the day but he refused until Bernard was sorted. He turned to the back page and frowned. "Wait here." A minute later he returned with a surprised mid-fifties man in a suit. "We need a witness."

Signatures placed, dated and observed, Scott pulled a bottle of wine out of the backpack. "Time to celebrate. Will you have a glass . . ." he looked down at the contract "Gerald?" Gerald stayed for a glass and then Scott and I finished the bottle. I'm an affectionate drunk. I thanked Scott over and over again for giving me my freedom.

"I couldn't have done it without you, I couldn't."

"Yeah, you could. Aren't you proud of yourself, the way you stood up to that jerk?"

I turned the word over in my mind a couple of times. That was it. The feeling I hadn't put a name to. I was proud.

Steven wasn't so impressed about picking me up and driving me home. The girls were already in their pyjamas, teddy bears hugged to their chests, looking uncertain as I swayed towards the car.

"Goodbye, goodbye!" I called as I left the café for the last time. "I won't be back tomorrow." I turned as I reached the passenger door and threw my keys at Scott. "She's all yours, Babe!"

That night I woke at 2 a.m. from a sweat-inducing nightmare, cornered by a monstrous cockroach in a hall of mirrors. I slipped out from under Steven's imprisoning arm and opened the balcony door, stepping out and gulping the cool air compulsively.

Once my heart slowed I leaned on the rail and let the gentle breeze play with my fringe, the satin of my nightgown pulled alternately around my legs and away. It was a mild autumn night; I had no desire to return to my nightmares.

Tiptoeing, I found socks and a warm robe and carried out a chair and my laptop. I would work on transcribing Wendy's interview. She had said she would like to work some of it into an article.

Soon, with the soothing flow of her positive, encouraging words my breath was even and my mood calm. Somehow the depth of repetitive listening – I'm not the quickest typist – intensified the Wendy experience, making it even more powerful. My optimism returned and I began making plans for ordering my home. It was funny how, even though I was focused on the task, there was a freedom of mind, a drifting sort of inspiration, like I've noticed before when painting the house, or wiping down tables at the end of a good day. Ideas began to form and reform, refining and transforming.

"It's more important that people know exactly what they want . . ." Wendy quoted, "than that they conform to someone else's ideal. I recommend taking a sheet of paper and writing down just that - if we're making changes, they may as well be the changes that inspire us. What do you want?" As I typed the question and replayed the quote it sunk down deep into my mind, echoing and repeating hypnotically. "What do I want? What do I want?"

I found myself yawning and at the same time the laptop beeped its battery warning. I crept back into bed and was soon fast asleep.

TASHA STUART INTERVIEWS . . .

7

It was a weird feeling to wake the next morning and have nothing planned for the day. I got up and made pikelets for the girls' breakfast, eating a large plateful myself. I told Steven I'd take them to school, which he normally did, and he left early for work, casting a curious look in my direction but asking no questions. I'd tell him my plans once I had some.

I sat in the car after walking Greta to class, hands on the wheel, staring out the windscreen. I could go anywhere, do anything. Six glorious hours of freedom. And feeling proud. No debt. No business payments to make. I'd like to contribute financially to the family, but I had time. I had time.

The street was deserted when I finally started the engine and pulled away from the curb. I felt like a drive, out of town. The petrol gauge showed full – I love that! Akaroa. Ice cream. Fish and chips. Walk along the seafront. Look in the shops.

Straight roads and dry, sculpted hills passing on my left. Passing the turning to Birdlings Flat with memories of a stony beach holiday in a broken down bach. Little River, where the line of cars all stopped to refresh themselves so that I began the winding hill climb with a clear road in front of me. "That's me," I thought, "I love having clear road in life, no one to follow, no one telling me how things should be." I'm a bit of a sucker for a good metaphor.

Cresting the hilltop between the two extinct volcanoes of Banks Peninsula you get an almost aerial view of Akaroa Harbour, Onawe Peninsula striking out into the water, a stepping stone view towards the further bays and Akaroa itself. The water changes mood from day-to-day, today almost black, boasting its cold depth, defying the bright blue of the sky.

Entering the town is a fresh contrast to the drama of the surrounding landscape, with the cheerful weatherboard houses and tongue-in-cheek references to the French heritage which the locals are secretly quite proud of.

The dairy next to the supermarket in Akaroa makes the best ice creams, still doing classic chocolate dip with original Tip Top Hokey Pokey ice cream. You have to eat the chocolate fast, especially on a hot day, before the ice cream melts and drips down the cone. I always hope no-one I know will come by before I have finished – I'm a girl who likes to focus on her food. I'd eat alone 90% of the time, from choice.

This time I spied an old friend just as I was finishing – perfect. We stood on the footpath and caught up on husbands and children and houses. She'd just bought a place here for holidays, a long forgotten dream of mine.

I turned in the direction of the sun and strolled along the Esplanade. At the other end of the town I stopped in at a gift shop and bought myself a straw hat. I felt so peaceful, dreamlike. I walked out on the pier and dangled my legs next to the old locals' fishing lines, feeling the breeze on my face again. I closed my eyes behind my sunglasses and turned my face up to the sunlight. Breath followed breath. I listened to the sea gulls' cries.

It's funny how motion comes without conscious warning. In a second, one foot was up under me and I was standing, teetering for a moment, then strolling back along the wooden boards. Perhaps it was a waft of hot oil smell – I was drawn to the fish and chip shop, turning back to the sea front with my paper-wrapped parcel, finding a blue painted seat on the edge of the harbour. My eyes strayed over close-moored yachts, wires dinging in the light wind. Gulls darted and dashed with increasing bravery on the ground around my feet. Sparrows kept out of their way.

I ate the fish but there were far more chips than I wanted. Once they had cooled a little I threw one to the waiting birds. A frenzy began, precipitating an excited pulse-shift as I watched. I tossed them faster and faster, higher and higher, realising I could choose a specific bird and watch the red rings around its eyes as chip met target beak. It was mesmerising, hypnotic, exhilarating to develop a new, completely unlooked-for skill. I knew Steven would be horrified by the flap of scores of wings so near but I felt powerful. The wrapper finally discarded, the birds one by one flew away.

I stared out over the water, completely content. It was like time had stopped, no movement, my stream of thought in lamina flow. My attention shifted with the roll of an airborne seagull's wings, tipping gently left and right in response to the shifting air currents. I felt like I could have anything I wanted. The concern for money had fallen out of my thoughts, leaving peace after years of turbulence. My face relaxed, my eyes closed. I breathed a deep breath in and let it go, feeling the beat of my heart steady and high in my chest. Peace.

TASHA STUART INTERVIEWS . . .

8

I pulled off my headphones as I put the final full stop to Wendy's completed transcript. I read it over, corrected a couple of spelling mistakes and wondered about the verbal grammatical style - it sounded fine but it didn't read like writing. Well, she could make that call. The audio was fantastic, so full of life and inspiration, it captured Wendy perfectly. I had suggested she take some sound bites to put on her website. She had made some suggestions for my website, in turn, and said I should get a separate phone line for the business. "Cute as it may be, you can't have a seven year old answering your phone."

She came over to pick up the CD with the files, smiling slightly as she took it and refusing to say why.

"Who are you going to do next?"

"Well . . ." I was a little nervous about asking anyone else. "Maybe my Dad."

She raised her eyebrows.

"He's had such an interesting life," I protested, "and I've never taken the time to hear much about it." That was true. I wondered aloud if all families were the same, so full of family dynamics that the one-on-one relationships slipped by.

"No," Wendy responded. "Not all families are like that. Okay, interview your dad, your mum, your uncles and aunts, why not? In the meantime, I'll make some calls."

"I'm still learning."

"While you're learning you might as well be doing."

"I'm not a professional yet."

She picked up the business cards I had had printed by her designer. "Yes you are, it says it here. 'Tasha Stuart, Professional Interviewer'." She put three of them in her bag. "I'll give you a call tomorrow."

There is always something left behind in the air after Wendy leaves a room. I find it stimulating, somewhat disquieting, and I can never just sit still, I have to take some action.

The night before, I had told Steven my plans. It had taken some courage, but to my surprise he thought it was a great idea.

"Think of all the people who are great at what they do, who have no arena to express it! What about chefs? People want to know a chef loves food, but where do they get to say it? You could interview them and put it on their websites – they could distribute it on CDs in the local neighbourhood. Just 30% more clientele would make a huge difference to most restaurants."

He was right. I wondered for a panging moment whether something like this would have saved the café. "Why didn't you say this before? I could have tried it myself!"

He has this expression sometimes which tells me I'm mad. It's always there and gone before I can say anything about it. My nose wrinkled and mouth twitched in protest, but, as always, it wasn't the time for that conversation.

My face echoed the same movements now unconsciously, but my thoughts were following the idea. Scott was passionate about cooking, and talking about a website. I could use him as a guinea pig. The designer who did my business cards could get the CDs made, I was sure. I looked at my watch. 1:30. He'd still be in the lunchtime rush. I sent him a text. "Call me later, I have an idea."

I sat with the phonebook in front of me, momentarily paralysed by fear. The list of restaurants was quite familiar, lots of well known names there. Should I start with the ones I knew or the ones I didn't? I had a better idea of what I would say to the ones I knew, but perhaps I should make my mistakes with the ones I didn't care so much about. For a moment I considered giving up on the phone altogether and going to each one. Way less efficient, but at least I wouldn't be facing this terrifying moment right now, I could put it off for a while. Wendy's advice echoed in my head. "Make five calls, then celebrate. It doesn't matter whether you get to talk to them or not, whether they say yes or not. Just dial five numbers and call it a success."

The voice in my own head argued that it would not be a success unless I got a sale. I put it aside. Not useful. Too much pressure. "And do you really want your self-worth determined by some random person you talk to on the phone?" Wendy again.

"No, I don't want it! But how can it be any other way?"

She rolled her eyes. "Stop procrastinating. Just get on with it. You'll be great."

Scott had had advice, too, after our interview. "This is fantastic! There are all sorts of people I can give this link to - I'm going for catering jobs, Christmas functions. I can't talk to everyone in each organisation, but if they want to hear me, here it is. Focus on the value you are offering. That way it gets the attention off you, onto the client, where it belongs."

Focus on the value I am offering. I referred to the script I had typed up and made a couple of changes.

My shaking finger dialled a number and I crossed it off with a pencil at the same time.

"Hi, this is Tasha Stuart. Am I speaking to the owner?"

"Well, when will she be in?"

"And her name is . . ?"

"Thanks . . . no, no message, I'll call back."

I hung up and felt like vomiting. Would I ever get through this? At the same time, I felt a little better. One down. After five I would take a stroll to the dairy and buy myself an ice cream to celebrate. Yes.

Dialling again.

"Hi, this is Tasha Stuart. Am I speaking to the owner?"

"Great! I'm calling because I am a professional interviewer specialising in profile interviews for restaurants. More and more people are going to the internet for information on restaurants, and a short interview with the owner or chef can give people a sense of the passion you bring to your food and service."

"You don't have a website?"

32

"Do you mind if I send you some information anyway, outlining my services?"

"And your address? Sorry, and I didn't catch your name?"

"Thanks so much for your time. Goodbye."

I leaned my head back on the chair, heart thumping slightly less this time. To give myself a break before picking up the phone again I took out an envelope and addressed it, folding the letter I had printed and putting a business card inside. Wendy had suggested a small gift, also, so I had bought some of those flat, individually wrapped Whittaker's chocolates; I put one of those in as well. I would post it in the box outside the dairy. Yes. I was beginning to feel in control.

Three more calls: two answer phones and a hang up. Okay, that's five. I picked up my bag, swinging it jauntily over my shoulder. I nodded firmly to myself. Time to celebrate.

TASHA STUART INTERVIEWS . . .

9

"Why is life such a rollercoaster?" I wailed at Wendy, a vision in swirling turquoise today.

She gave me a half smile and stepped out to speak to a prospective client. We were staffing the Women in Business stand at the Women's Lifestyle Expo, free to talk about our own businesses at the same time as inviting new members. Wendy did both adeptly. I tried to emulate her, hurling myself out into the concourse in the path of the oncoming hordes, and very quickly had to retire injured with no result - there hadn't been time to attempt a reproduction of her charm and calm.

"Don't bother with the ones who won't meet your eye. Wait for the ones who show interest."

It was a subtlety which was lost on me unless they walked right up to the table. Wendy's book was on display, so I found myself promoting her business more than mine. Once we got talking it was easier, though; once I was revving enthusiasm about Wendy it was easier to sound positive about myself. With one ear on her conversation, too, I got ideas for things to say.

"How long have you been a member?" the shorter and more stylish of two women asked me.

"Not long, but it's a great way to meet other women in business. And networking is a great way to grow your client base." As if I knew, after two meetings and a ladies lunch. "Do you have a business of your own?"

"I have a hair salon."

"Great! And you?"

"Not yet, just thinking about it."

"Well, why not try it? You can come along to a couple of meetings before you decide whether to join or not. Here, let me give you a flier."

Wendy leaned past me to pick up a book. "You're doing great!" she whispered.

I grinned back at her. She always lifts my confidence. But how can anyone do this for any length of time? After 90 minutes I just wanted to poke people in the eye.

Finally we were relieved and went in search of coffee. "Can't we go outside? I can't stand this noise any more." Wendy firmly steered me through the crowd and sat me at a table. "Use the cone of silence," she recommended. "Long black coffee?"

"And cake. I need cake."

I sat with my hands over my ears until she returned.

"Now, what was that about a rollercoaster?"

"Oh, God!" I took a sip of coffee, way too hot, and spluttered, trying to keep my mouth closed as it burned my lips, tongue and throat. She handed me her water bottle and wiped spots of coffee from the table.

"Well?"

I gave a deep sigh. "Oh, I was so looking forward to today – if only I'd known! – you know, a chance to be a grownup, real marketing, I felt like the business was real for the first time. And then Charlotte got sick, needed to stay home from school, and Steven and I got into this big fight. When I had the café I could ask Scott to come in early, or just get Steven to cover with the children until I'd done the morning setup, but today I asked him to stay home the whole morning. You know what he said?"

Wendy raised her eyebrows. "I think I can tell by your face, but let me hear it."

"He said 'Look, Tasha, I have a real job. I can't just take the morning off to babysit.'"

"And?"

"And I was furious. I said 'It's not called babysitting, it's called parenting. And how am I going to make it a real job if every time one of the kids has a sniffle I have to change my plans? I said I'd be there today. If I don't go it makes me look unprofessional!' "

"And then?"

"I slammed out, took Greta and Erica to school, just left him there with Charlotte. I was boiling, but I felt horrible, too, for losing it, for upsetting the kids by shouting, for making Charlotte feel bad for being sick.

"Then I got a text saying 'Sorry. I'll take her to my mum's. I have a meeting I can't miss but I'll pick her up after that.' I know he's great, really. I'm such a mess. And I was feeling so wonderful yesterday, so proud of myself, like I was really on my way."

"So do you need to go home now?"

I looked at my watch. "No, I said I'd be back by 1. I need to unwind a little first." I put my head down on the table. "I'm never going to make this work."

"No, you're probably right. Take your shoes to Goodwill, you won't need them with your heated kitchen floor."

I laughed, raised a sardonic eyebrow. "How do you always know just the right thing to say?"

"Let's take a spin through the show, see if we can't drum up some more business."

She was like a whirlwind, stopping at every stand. "Are you the owner? Looks like a great business - do you have a card? Look, I know you haven't got time to talk now, but here's my flier, and my friend's, I'm Wendy Rob-Williams and this is Tasha Stuart. Give us a call if you'd like to talk some more." I watched her: fliers with left hand, handshake with right hand, take their card, warm eye contact and gone. People watched her as she walked away, then they turned over the fliers in their hands with interest. Wow! And she loved it, she thrived on it. I was a jelly, just watching.

"How do you do that?"

"How? I just do it. It works. You watch, there'll be some calls tomorrow."

And she was right. That was how I got my first paid interview.

10

When I got home the phone was ringing. I picked it up automatically as I walked through the kitchen, grimacing my apology to Steven and not looking at the caller ID.

"Mum. Hi," Damn, I should have left it, connected properly with Steven, checked on Charlotte and called her back later. "How are you?" I checked through a pile of mail as she gave me the run down, possibly cutting herself a little short as I grunted my responses without really listening. Then she said something that caught my attention. "Kate's coming home?" I repeated. "When? For how long?"

Permanently. I love my sister, I really do. I tried to smile as I turned to Steven to tell him the news, but the sinking feeling broke through into startling consciousness.

"Kate's coming home. To live."

"That's great!" The shine in his eyes was the worst part. He loves her. She's just like me only better, and so charming with him, with all my boyfriends. So carefree and casual as she drops smiles like she's breaking a pearl necklace, so that the beads bounce and tinkle on the floor, causing mayhem and disaster for me as I skid and slide on them for a long time after. No-one knows me as well as she does – do I imagine the subtle undermining, the accidental exposure of my most tender flaws? I fade, bleeding and invisible, into the background as everyone gathers and coos. Perhaps I'm over-reacting. I do have a tendency to do that.

I curled up on the sofa next to Steven and looked over at where Charlotte was sleeping. "How is she?"

"She's been sick a couple of times, but not for a couple of hours. I gave her an ice block to suck on, and she's had a sip of water or two since." He pointed to the cup.

"And how are you? Was it okay coming home from work?"

"Yeah, sure." He's an angel really. I keep reminding myself I just need to wait through his irritation at any change of plan, he always comes around after a while.

"Sorry I yelled."

He shook his head.

"We're fine now, if you want to get back to work."

"Yeah, I'll do that. Want me to make you something to eat first?"

"No, I'm fine. I'll get something later."

"I'll give you a call when I'm coming home."

I watched Charlotte's breath rise and fall. She looked much younger than twelve, peaceful, but with her straight bob clinging to the sweat on her neck.

All three girls have the same heart shaped face, pretty pointed chin, wide eyes. I guess they get those from me. Erica and Greta have Steven's blue eyes, while Charlotte tends more to my hazel. The two younger girls have Steven's curls too, Erica's wilder than Greta's gentle waves.

Charlotte opened her eyes and smiled at me. "Hi, Mum. How did it go?"

"It was great, but I'm glad to be back with you now. Want some water?"

She nodded and I passed her the cup. She drank a little and passed it back, hand shaking.

"You hungry?"

"No."

"Want to watch a movie?"

"Maybe, yeah."

I gave her a pile of DVDs to choose from and went to fetch her a blanket. She stretched out on the sofa and I sat on the floor beside her as the music began. Twilight. Just time to watch it before the younger girls came home.

TASHA STUART INTERVIEWS . . .

11

It was silly but I really wanted to have a paid interview under my belt before I told Kate about my new business. The enquiry phone call the next day was a god-send, and I was so eager to make it work I had to fight back serious impulses to discount, to express inappropriate gratitude and to beg. Somehow I held it together and the time was set for the following Thursday. "Please, let the kids be well!" I prayed as I turned the small conservatory into a relatively professional recording studio. It hadn't seemed to matter as much when it was Wendy, but now I took down the family photographs and moved the last of the children's toys back out to their bedroom.

The recorder and microphones were out but not assembled - I liked the idea of doing this as we talked, to put the subject at ease: while I was unwinding cords and connecting microphones it was clear we were just chatting, not "waiting to start."

The subject was Marlene and she was the owner of a women's gym. She wanted a short promotional CD to hand out at networking meetings. She was excited on the phone. "I know how often I just throw away a business card, not being able to remember the person who gave it to me - that's why I've got my picture on mine - but a CD is novel, will raise curiosity and also promise and deliver real information." I wrote that down and asked if I could use it in my marketing material. "Sure, I'll give you a testimonial, too, if you like, once we're done."

I'm a great believer in letting the unconscious work on things for a couple of days before tackling them for real, so I asked her to think about what she'd like to say. I based my questions on Malcolm Gladwell's "The Tipping Point," where he talks about people he calls connectors.

"Your potential clients want to know what you do, what you're really good at and what you are passionate about."

"Say that again, slower?"

Marlene listened closely, and then, as with Wendy, it was like magic, the enthusiasm was pouring out. I'm an inveterate non-exerciser, and she almost had even me thinking about joining her gym. I held firm, though, I know my propensity to jump at every good idea and never follow through. Well, not never . . .

I made some notes from what she was saying, so I could be sure we covered it again when we recorded. A private theory I have, which I don't share with clients, is that enthusiasm, and the resulting dopamine in the bloodstream which brings people alive, is contagious.

You know what it's like when you're in a room with someone who is really excited by something – it could be anything: ornithology or train spotting or travel or whatever – and they're waving their arms around. You catch it, you feel like it's you, you feel great. My theory was that this contagious nature of passion could transmit by recorded voice as well. If I could bring out the excitement, get the interviewee to experience that dopamine rush, it would change the world of anyone listening. That's what the aim was, to communicate that. The content was secondary - actually largely irrelevant.

When I hear that passion, feel that contagious dopamine, I want to work with the person, regardless of what they do. As evidenced by the gym-temptation, which I was NOT going to give in to.

"So, ever thought of joining a gym?"

"Well, I . . ."

"Why not come in for a free session, just to see what it's like. I'll leave your name at reception, come in any time."

Well, why not, if it was free? She did make it sound like fun. And I'd be able to tell Kate when she asked what exercise I was doing.

"I have a client who owns a gym," I could hear myself saying. "So there are free sessions there." I decided to make a point of going before August the 12th.

"So do you have everything you need?" Marlene asked.

My final technique was to introduce the expectation of success. "Yes, great, and now you've talked this through, it will be effortless on the day. You don't even need to think about it before then, just come along, you'll be fantastic, just as inspiring as you've been today."

Yeah!

12

I was rushing to get Marlene's transcript and edited audio done before picking Kate up from the airport. I wanted to deliver the disk on my way, not least because the terms of my contract were credit card payment on receipt of the files, so that meant I would get paid.

"What time does her flight arrive?"

"Steven, I'm trying to get this done. Not for half an hour."

"But you'll want to get there and park."

I screwed up my hands and tried to block him out. Just one more minute of interview to go, but each one was taking nine or ten minutes to edit and transcribe, then I had to write the CD. I was cutting it fine.

"Tasha?"

"She'll have to get through customs, wait for her bags." "And find some hapless male to help her lift them onto the trolley, heaven forbid she should strain herself." I added in a whisper. I really was looking forward to her coming, but everyone else was making such a fuss. I knew now what the brother of the prodigal son felt like, only it was probably worse for me, because Kate hadn't been the same sort of shit before she left as the biblical traveller.

"Is she staying here?"

I looked up at him in amazement, and around at our chaotic, tiny house. "No," I said shortly, concentrating on my keyboard again. "She's staying at Mum's until she finds a place. Sweetheart, I can't do this and talk to you at the same time, and I need to get it done."

"You'll be late."

I clenched my teeth. "I need to get it done." I should have taken my laptop upstairs but it was too late to relocate now. I sometimes felt like I was teetering on the edge of sanity, close to causing violent harm to one of my loved ones when they interrupted me for the 20th time in an hour. "I'm serious, Steven. Just go."

I closed my eyes as he withdrew. I knew I had hurt him, that he didn't understand. Focus.

Yay! The credit was easy and the last 15 seconds were clunks and clicks and 'thank you's. It was done. Save, render to MP3, plug in the CD drive, blank disk, write the .wav, .mp3 and .doc to the disk. No time to print an image on the CD, but she'd just copy it off anyway. I stuck my business card to the outside of the case with Sellotape and ran for the door.

I dropped the disk at Marlene's reception at a run, guaranteed the least fit person there, panting from the single flight of stairs and barely able to tell the receptionist who it was for.

I was panting as I ran into the arrivals lounge, too, just as Kate breezed through the door pushing her trolley full of Vuitton luggage and laughing beautifully at the bronzed god next to her.

Any snapshot of Kate could be captioned with the words "Beautiful woman . . ." "Beautiful woman strolls though airport" "Beautiful woman braves supermarket" "Beautiful woman walks in comparatively shabby native bush." And she always looks happy. Until we're alone, that is, when she drops the façade, or rather replaces it with another one, the "I'm really jealous of you, you know" pre-emptive strike. I'd hate her if I didn't love her. Actually, I think I do hate her. But that doesn't mean I don't love her as well.

I watched her flick her long blond hair over her shoulder and laugh once more, squeezing Adonis' arm good-bye before turning towards me and holding out her arms.

"Tasha! It's so good to see you!" and there were real tears in her eyes. That hug felt real, too, not just a perfunctory air kiss but full body to body contact and real love flooding through me. "I've missed you so much."

Intense feeling welled up through me, releasing 20 different things at once. "There's so much I want to talk to you about. I'm so glad you're home." And after all the negative anticipation, the resentment, the jealousy, in this moment of just the two of us, I really was.

That's another thing about Kate: you really feel it's just the two of you, until she turns from you and then it's just her and someone else, and you're left in the cold.

I took the trolley from her. Adonis was still lingering. Kate turned back towards him. "Hey," he said, "you're like, twins." Kate grinned, I grimaced.

"We are twins! Sharp lad! Thanks so much for the help." She turned and took a few steps towards the door, and then she did it, her signature move. She spun on her heel back to face him, arms up under her long blonde hair, then brought them up to the top of her head, letting the hair fall back to her shoulders again. A laugh, another 180 degree turn and she continued walking towards the door. I've seen guys watch her down a whole street to see if she'll do it again.

Genetically, we're identical. And that's where it stops.

"Can we go see Mum and Dad before we go back to your place?"

"My place?"

"Yeah - I want to see Greta and Erica and Charlotte and Steven. Of course I do! And I want to hear all about what you're doing since you sold the café. There's so much to catch up on."

Hmm.

We dropped off the luggage; I watched my parents' joy at welcoming Kate home, their sadness when she got back in my car again.

"Did you hear Mum's accent? Please tell me I never talked like that."

"Kate!" I had noticed her new posh English voice and thought it sounded false.

"What? You know I'd never say anything to anyone but you - but wow! It's awful!"

I said nothing. I wasn't getting pulled into this.

"You're still in the same house! Cool."

We walked into the living room and the girls came running. They love their Auntie Kate, she spoils them with presents and will spend hours sitting on the floor with them playing their games. She always was a girlie girl and I've never quite understood their fascination with dolls. Steven's face lit up, too. She leaned over Greta to kiss his cheek. I saw him put a hand to it afterwards. "How are you?"

"Just fine!"

I made lunch and we ate in the conservatory, new since Kate's last visit. I was fighting with the girls trying to get some salad on their plates while Steven and Kate carried on the adult conversation at the other end of the table.

"So, did you leave any heartbroken men on the other side of the world?"

She shrugged. "No-one irreplaceable. I'm back on the prowl now I'm here, though, let me know if you run into anyone suitable."

"Which would be . . ?"

"Tall, fit, rich, with a forgiving nature – you know me."

Steven caught her eye and laughed. "Do I? I think you've changed."

"For the better?"

He didn't answer. "You're looking for a job?"

"Yeah, I should be. Think I'll take a couple of weeks off first, though, I really deserve a holiday." She stretched her arms up like a cat, accentuating her long, slim torso.

He nodded. Erica knocked over her juice – or was it me? I really wasn't paying attention to anything much, Greta had three slices of bread on her plate – we'd be lucky if she ate one – and had mashed her tomato into pulp. Now Erica was screaming. There was juice on the party dress she had put on especially for Kate. I moved things away from the flood and looked up.

"Steven, will you get a cloth!"

He slowly turned from Kate and saw what was happening. It took him a moment to work out what to do and head for the kitchen, but Charlotte had beaten him to it, running back into the room with a tea towel.

Kate came around the table and pulled Erica into a sticky hug. "It's okay, Darling. Let's go find you something else to wear."

I took the towel from Charlotte and handed it to Steven. I could barely look at him as we sorted the mess together.

"Did you get any on you, Charlotte?"

"No."

"Then go with Greta to the living room, we'll take care of this." I turned my back on Steven and started clearing the table.

Kate and Erica returned, Erica all smiles, her long curls flowing over a new pink Girl Power t-shirt. "Look Mummy, Auntie Kate brought me a present."

"It was supposed to be for later, but I thought the need was greater now," she said in response to my raised eyebrows. She took her plate out of my hands, "Hey, I wasn't finished!" She curled up in an armchair and picked at her meal while the girls brought their treasures to show her. Steven turned on the TV. My hands got angrier and angrier in the hot water as I washed up alone.

13

I was quickly learning how transcribing and editing the audio of an interview could calm me down, get me out of my own head and into somebody else's. A 30 minute interview with one of the National Speakers' guys had turned into 45 minutes of fascination and as I listened to the soft lull of his voice over and over again I reached a still, meditative state that I have never achieved before, any other way.

Sometimes an idea would grab me, show me a way forward through my own life; sometimes the clean repetition he used for effect and emphasis took me deeper into an hypnotic state as my fingers learned the sequence of character keys.

I was also fascinated by the cadence of speech, the patterns which emerged in such a close examination – or not an examination: that sounded too conscious. What I was doing was like the difference between walking a route and driving it: you see more, feel more, are closer to everything. In the end it is part of you in a way a driven road never is.

Today I was using the task of editing to shut out my jealousy. I knew I was over-reacting. They were only flirting. Kate probably wouldn't see it as even that. 'Although,' I thought bitterly, 'I'm sure Steven would like to.' I felt like such a drudge by comparison. There she was, single and carefree, no responsibilities, nothing to do, except . . .

"I thought I'd hang out with you."

"I've got work to do."

"Well, I'll help. What is it?"

"Marketing mostly, difficult and dull, I'm sure you'd rather be shopping."

"Marketing? Dull? I love it! A chance to talk to people about something exciting and new. Tell me more about what you're doing . . ."

I closed my mind again and tried to focus on the recorded words. I didn't want to think that here was yet another thing she was better at than me. I'd managed to convince her to have coffee with a friend, but she would be back in an hour or so, to make some marketing calls for me. I'd have to listen, and feel more inadequate. Maybe I'd find an excuse to go out.

"You're behaving badly," said the voice in my head.

"I know."

"She's trying to be helpful."

"I know."

"And you never know, she could really make a difference, get you going, make this a success."

"I know! Shut up." And I felt horrible. Would I really rather fail than have Kate to thank for my success? Apparently so.

When it came to it, it was inspiring listening to Kate on the phone. I pretended to have some filing to do – in fact I really did have lots of filing to do, but I never actually do it, so there's no way that's what I would have been doing now in any other circumstance. To my surprise the filing process felt very similar to the transcribing, relaxing as it consumed my focus but left part of my mind free to roam.

Punch holes in the stack of invoices; check the date and file in alphabetic order. Wendy had designed my filing system and had made it very simple for me. Only this time I had mixed up invoices for the old business and the new one, which made it a little more complicated.

My accountant would shake her head, but she was fantastic, too, great at working with what she had. "Don't worry, you do what you're good at, I'll do what I'm good at. Just make sure you keep everything." So I had this big file of receipts which I normally just dumped on her desk every couple of months. She'd get a surprise this time, when she saw the ordered folder.

I paused when I heard Kate dialling.

"Hi, am I speaking to the owner of the company?"

She sounded so bright and positive. I recalled my own timidity and shaking voice. In her words, my interview service sounded enticing even to me. Maybe I should do a sound-clip myself. I wondered why I hadn't thought of it before.

She put her hand over the phone. "Give me your calendar."

"My what?"

"Your calendar. He wants to make a booking."

I stared at her. I hadn't thought it through this far. "I don't know, any time Friday, or next week between 9 and 3."

She rolled her eyes. "She has a gap on Friday at 10:30 or next Tuesday at 1 p.m."

"Tuesday? Great. The address is 129 Forster St. Tasha will call you on Friday to discuss what you'd like to say. Would 9 o'clock be convenient? Fantastic! Have a great day!"

She turned around beaming.

"You got one? You got one? That was only your third call!"

"Yeah."

I jumped up and hugged her, feeling only the tiniest twinge of ungrateful chagrin. She was already picking up the phone again. "Okay, onwards we go."

We sat laughing with a glass of wine. Kate had made ten appointments before I could convince her to stop. Something had changed in me, listening to her confidence, in herself, but also in me. I thought I could do it more easily myself now, and I felt happy and free.

Now she was regaling me with stories of England, working in a pub as she saved money for travelling. "You know me, I don't like to be tied down to serious work. I wanted to be free in the mornings for sightseeing, and I wanted to meet people – fun people, not suits full of ambition. They might not have been the highest calibre, but, boy, we had some laughs."

"I don't know if I could handle it, working in a bar. What do you do if someone gets drunk and unpleasant?"

She shrugged. "Tell them to go. Ask the bouncer to deal with them. But always with a smile. You know everyone loves me." She stuck out her tongue like she did when we were kids. I found myself punching her like I did back then, when I thought she was getting above herself. We both shrieked with laughter.

"Oh no! It's three o'clock, and I'm in no state to drive. Want to walk down with me and pick up the girls?"

I got their scooters out of the garage to minimise the moan factor when they saw I didn't have the car. Kate took Erica's and fiddled with the wing nuts. "How does it work?"

"You're not going to ride it?"

"Why not?"

I had no answer, so I opened out two of the scooters and pulled the handles to full height. Which wasn't very high. Then we wobbled and laughed along the footpath, Kate coming to a swinging halt at the corner as a car skimmed her back wheel. "Dangerous," she observed seriously, then doubled up with laughter.

"Shh!" I said. We were approaching the school gate and some of the other mothers were turning to stare.

TASHA STUART INTERVIEWS . . .

14

"I've invited Bernard to dinner tonight."

I froze, gazing blankly at Steven as he sipped beer from the bottle, leaning in the kitchen doorway.

Kate looked up. "Great! I'd love to see him again." She was preparing a salad. I knew the girls would eat it: it had flowers in it.

Steven flicked me a look. "That's cool then." He sauntered back to the living room.

I turned on Kate as soon as he was gone. "Great? How can you say that? The guy's a creep!"

"Oh, I don't know. I've always had a bit of a thing for him since that bridesmaid-best man moment." She smiled a secret smile into the lettuce.

"Don't tell me . . ?"

"It was nothing. You know I'm a sucker for that bad boy façade. It'll be cool to see him again."

I sighed a whoosh of air and rolled my eyes up towards my lowered forehead.

"Come on, he's fun!"

"He's dishonest and cruel and lecherous."

"Well, so am I, sometimes."

I turned my head away from her in frustration. "You are not!"

"Well, not usually all three at once. But I know it's there, in me. It's fun to explore it. Admit it! You've got it, too."

"Me!"

"Jung says we should embrace the shadow."

"Why? Why should I?"

"Like I said, it's fun. It gives you freedom."

"I don't want that sort of freedom."

"It gives you freedom to be who you choose to be. If you hold it in too hard it will come out in other ways. Ways you can't control."

"That's ridiculous. What ways?"

"Like being a grumpy bitch all the time."

I narrowed my eyes and stared into hers. For a moment they were black and hard, then she laughed. "Let me pour you another glass of wine. You take life way too seriously."

I was so angry I couldn't speak. I wanted to throw her out but I knew I'd just look like the villain.

Bernard arrived and the girls ran to him just like they did to Kate. He tickled them and threw them in the air and I wanted to see something sinister in it but it really did look like fun. They shrieked and pulled his hair and then finally sat quiet on his knee while he ogled Kate. "Hi, Gorgeous. Good to see you back." The bluff confidence was gone now and there was something of the awkward schoolboy in the way he responded to her welcoming kiss. "Here for long?"

"Charlotte, Greta, would you help me carry these out to the table?" I knew I'd never untangle Erica from the centre of the action.

Bernard looked through the serving hatch as the girls slipped off his knee. "Hi Tasha." There was an awkward expression in his eyes, as if he was unsure of his reception.

"Hi." I leaned sideways for him to kiss my cheek as I carried two plates of meat out.

"Sorry," he whispered. "I was a bit of an ass."

My mouth opened but I could think of nothing to say; he was turning away anyway.

"Tasha, what else is there?" Kate called.

"Your salad, and the bread."

I helped Greta up onto the seat next to mine and busied myself making sure she got something sensible to eat. When I looked up Steven was watching me warily. I gave him a weak half smile.

Bernard and Kate sat either side of Charlotte, across from Erica, and acted up for their entertainment, the noise escalating as they tried to outdo each other. Soon we were all laughing, but I had a lump in my chest that I couldn't shift. Dessert over, we moved towards the living room.

"Sing for us, Uncle Bernard!"

It was always a surprise seeing the ex-league player at the piano. His shoulders seemed to fill the width of the keyboard and his fingers looked too broad to fit between the keys.

Kate looked up from her magazine with interest and I watched her mouth drop and stay open as Bernard sang. Steven came and sat beside me on the sofa. He took my hand and appeared to be absorbed in the song but there was a spark of dissatisfaction in his eye.

"Now your turn," said Bernard. "Have you been practising that song I taught you on Charlotte's birthday?"

I had heard Charlotte, Erica and Greta singing along to the CD player in their room but hadn't paid much attention. Now it was my turn to drop my jaw as they stood up next to the piano stool – "Face the audience, that's right" – and sang.

I recognised the song, "So What?" from my favourite Lilac album. I wanted to disapprove but it was really pretty cute. Kate jumped up and danced in front of them, showing them actions which they copied with delight. For six, eight and twelve they were fabulous singers. They didn't get that from me. Steven squeezed my hand and flashed me a beaming smile. That felt good until I saw his eyes rest for longer and longer on Kate instead of on his daughters.

The song finished and we applauded loudly, but I was still out of sorts. "Come on, Charlotte, Erica, Greta, time for bed."

"Oh, Mum! You're just a spoil-sport," Erica accused, eyes dark with anger. "You always spoil the fun." Charlotte and Greta were glaring, too. A tear rose in the corner of my eye.

"I'll give you a piggyback." Bernard picked up Greta and galloped a circle around the room before heading down the hall. Kate grabbed Erica and carried her, squealing, by the ankles.

"Put your hands down, I'm dropping you!" Kate shrieked and Erica turned the corner to their bedroom in a supported handstand. "Coming, Charlotte?"

"I'll read them a story." I said, and followed them out.

Pyjamas on and teeth and hair brushed the atmosphere in the bedroom became quiet and peaceful. "Snuggle down. Where's the book?"

We had been reading "Harry Potter" and the chapters were long. It suited me to take refuge here for a while. The adult voices were a quiet murmur in the distance and I allowed my face to relax into a long low sadness as I read.

"Mum! Do the voices!"

There were so many characters it took some concentration to keep their speech distinct. I forgot everything else and was soon immersed in the story. "Another chapter!"

I looked at my watch. "Not tonight, it's getting late." Reluctantly I pulled my arms from around Greta and Erica and jollied them into their own beds. I kissed them each on the forehead. "Good night, sweethearts."

"Can Uncle Bernard and Auntie Kate come and say goodnight."

"Kate will be here tomorrow."

"But Uncle Bernard hardly ever comes!"

"Well, I'll ask him to look in at the door. Snuggle down, now. Time to sleep."

TASHA STUART INTERVIEWS . . .

15

I loved the way interviewing took me out of myself. I was even more clear now that the key to success on a piece-by-piece basis, was bringing out the passion of the interviewee, getting their enthusiasm and inspiration running.

It was easy, actually. The first thing was, to turn around the idea that the subject's passion is contagious and generate this state in myself. That was simple, I loved what I was doing, listening to someone else's ideas. And once I had it, it transferred immediately to them, became an upward spiral, a natural high.

The second thing is, that almost anyone who has their own business started it with passion. It would have been something they were excited about. So I started with questions about why they chose this business, and took them back to the very beginning when there was guaranteed to be excitement – otherwise they would never have got going in the first place.

Third, I primed them with questions that expected highly positive answers: "What is the most inspiring aspect of what you offer your customers?" "What is the thing you love most about what you do?"

I figured the way to get good at this was just to do it. Kate was generating paid interviews, but I wanted more experience, so I contacted some of the people from the National Speakers' Association and asked if they would let me interview them. "No charge, and you could use the audio on your website. The transcript you might want to rework into an article, or submit it to a suitable publication as is - the interview format works well, and adds credibility."

The response was positive, and today I was interviewing Rupert Cooper about his coaching business. He arrived at the door. I was nervous, repeating my mantra: "Treat them like a star."

We chatted as I unravelled the microphones and set up the recorder. We had talked a couple of days before about the content of today's interview, it was well covered material for Rupert, his signature keynote speech. I had notes about what he planned to say and critical points to cover, but I had a feeling I wouldn't need it. I was already learning the difference between interviewing professional speakers and people who weren't - the professionals were much more fluent and I just got to listen and ask them to expand on areas which interested me. It was easy and fun.

With people who weren't used to speaking I sometimes needed to remind them of material they had left out, but that was easy and natural, too.

We agreed an introduction and started. All self-consciousness floated away and 35 minutes later I came back to awareness of myself like I'd been on holiday. Rupert was smiling broadly, nodding. I put in my final credit "Rupert Cooper was interviewed by professional interviewer Tasha Stuart www.tashastuart.co.nz" and we were done.

We thanked each other and I asked a question or two about his immediate plans, but I knew already from experience that I needed to get him out as fast as was polite. With Wendy, I had altered the mood after the mic was off, reacting to the outward focus by doing a big blurt about myself. I know this about me, this was why I had created this business, after all: because I have the tendency to talk too much about myself. I wanted Rupert gone before I switched modes and spoiled the afterglow.

Maybe I should get a journal to absorb the backlash – some of the thoughts spinning in my head looking for an exit were worth noting.

We exchanged another warm smile as he walked down the drive. I had a sense of privilege of having the opportunity to be one-on-one with such a fascinating person. And what was magical was that I knew I felt the same about everyone I interviewed.

Through the ups and downs of the next few days I took refuge in the editing and transcribing. In time I would look for someone to transcribe, but for now I loved it as a way of taking a break from whatever was going on in and around me. It helped my thoughts, too. I often found answers to things I was thinking about in the deep penetration of the content I was working with. This was becoming addictive, and very, very satisfying.

TASHA STUART INTERVIEWS . . .

16

"Okay, you have three interviews on Monday, can you handle that?"

"Three!"

"Two on Tuesday and one on Thursday. So far. You need to do the pre-interviews for Monday today or tomorrow. Here's the list."

"Oh my god! All paying clients?"

"Of course." Kate smiled at my expression. "I know, I'm fantastic. You can take me out for lunch."

My mouth hung open. "I could never have done this myself."

"I know." Kate repeated. "By the way, I've started taking credit card details when I make the booking. I figure it's easier then, and with some of them I wanted a way to get firm commitment. 24 hour notice of cancellation required otherwise they will be charged anyway. How's that?"

I was only half listening. "What does this mean?" I pointed to a column to the right of the names and contact details.

"That's the length of interview. 10 minutes for the standard self-promotion, 35 for CDs and this guy wanted an hour, to give more sense of value. He's going to use it as a value-add to his coaching clients."

"Coaching clients?" I felt like I was way behind.

"Yeah. I was talking to this restaurant owner, here, he was really excited, said he had been looking for something to set his website apart. He suggested I call his business coach, so this is him. I said you'd do the hour for the same price as the 35 minute – that ok?"

"Ok?" I hugged her, almost crying. I would never think a bad thought about her again.

"Come on, Drama Queen!" She smiled a sparkling smile. "Put on your best party dress. Let's do that lunch."

As I looked distractedly through my closet for anything with a hint of glamour I was calculating in my head. I turned away from the rack of clothes to the list on my bed. "Kate!" I called downstairs to the kitchen, where I could hear her washing up from breakfast.

"Yeah?"

"Have I made a mistake? Does this add up to $2,250 in one week?"

She appeared at the bottom of the stairs. "So far."

"Wow!" I could hardly take it in. "I could never, never have done this by myself."

"Yes, you could, if you just got over yourself. It's a great idea. People love it."

I shook my head, then spoke before the thought had half formed in my head. "Maybe we should go into partnership, you doing marketing, running the business, me doing the interviews?"

"God no! Never borrow money or go into business with family. Besides, me, own a business? You know my attention span, even the thought of it makes me freak out."

Her words were a relief. What had I been thinking? If only I had had her to advise me before I borrowed money from Bernard. Come to think of it, I do recall her saying something at the time.

"Look, I'm having fun, but pretty soon I'll get bored. So don't thank me too soon. You know I'll just let you down."

I ran downstairs and hugged her. "Too late. Now help me choose something to wear."

After lunch we went shopping. Kate got me to try on things I would never have picked out myself.

"I feel ridiculous! I don't even know how to move in this."

"Try leading from the hips. You're holding your weight higher, it makes you awkward. Think of your centre in your hips."

I considered taking offence for a second but then just tried it. "Hey!" I exclaimed, "It works. I feel sexy!"

She laughed, a loud, brief shout. "A miracle. So buy it!"

And I did.

TASHA STUART INTERVIEWS . . .

17

I dressed with some trepidation. Things had been a little strained between Steven and I – something was on his mind and we hadn't been alone for more than a few minutes in weeks. This fifteen year anniversary seemed important, like I had to get it right or there might not be another fifteen.

Looking at myself in the mirror I sighed. I was wearing the new dress Kate had picked out and I looked more like her than myself. I had put on makeup and found an old, simple necklace; my hair was in a chignon. I felt like a fraud.

Kate had taken the girls to Mum's to give me space to get ready and here I was with an hour to spare. I had forgotten what it was like not to be interrupted. Somewhere along the road of child raising I had developed some awesome efficiency, making the most of every streamlined motion, totally focused on what I was doing. Now what was I going to do with all this time? Steven wasn't even home yet.

I slid open the outside door and stepped onto the tiny balcony which had sold me the house, but which I only used twice a year. The sun was glancing down on enough of an angle to glide under the eaves and hit my face. How did I want the evening to go?

Sometimes, when the kids were really small, when I was tired, feeling unattractive and out of control, and wondering why Steven would even walk in the door amongst the chaos at the end of the day, I thought I'd lost what I felt for him in the beginning. The only way I could hold onto myself and what I wanted, was to imagine he was no longer there, that he had left me, or died. The deep, sharp pain I felt at the thought told me I still loved him, the feeling was just buried, there to be excavated when I had energy and time.

I applied the same technique now, quickly overwhelming myself with jealousy and grief. I sagged against the balustrade and let the tears flow, feeling cleaned out and hollow at the same time.

I heard a step behind me. Steven saw my streaked face and recoiled. "Babe, what's wrong?" I heard an edge of disapproval in the question. I knew I'd been awful. Steven likes home to be uncomplicated, so he can concentrate on the important things.

I stepped back into the bedroom. "Just give me a hug. I feel like we've been apart for a long time."

He put his arms tentatively around me, and as I relaxed into him, cheek pressed against his chest, he relaxed, too, and held me tighter. "I really do love you. Just sometimes I get confused." I extricated my arms from between our chests and wrapped them around him. He gave me a final squeeze. Time's up. I let him go, leaning back and smiling bravely. I realised it had been a long time since I looked him in the eye.

"I'll have a shower. What time do we need to go?"

I fixed my makeup while the water ran and went downstairs to let him dress in peace. There was a time when I would have stayed to watch, but I felt too exposed to do that now. Maybe I'd try my interview technique at dinner, shut up and let him talk. I smiled to myself. Now that would be a new thing. I wondered if it would work.

TASHA STUART INTERVIEWS . . .

18

It's always easier to run with an old pattern. It felt distinctly awkward leaving gaps for Steven to talk into. He even asked me if I was okay, and finally resorted to asking me the questions which would usually be unnecessary.

"Did you have a good day?"

"Mmm. You?"

"Yes." He looked at me out of the corner of his eye. "How are the interviews going?"

I was torn. He didn't usually show much interest in what I was doing professionally. It was a constant dull disappointment for me which I told myself I didn't notice any more. On the other hand I was trying to draw him out.

"Great, I love them. I think I may have found my calling. I learn so much and I love finding my way into each person's voice as I edit." I saw his eyes glaze over as my enthusiasm warmed despite my intention. Wow, that hurt. I felt a tug on my upper right cheek, under the outside of my eye. There was a corresponding stone-drop sensation behind my solar plexus. I pulled the shutters down hard on the window I had opened and took a sip of champagne, to recover myself. Damn. Champagne didn't go with this feeling.

Steven never talked about his plans and hopes. He was always steady, no visible risks, no disappointments. Whereas my life could be a thrilling rollercoaster of excitement and plans and wild new experience, his looked, from the outside, like an antique steam train ride over a long plain. At least, my life used to be like that. Somewhere along the way I had lost my stomach for failure. I used to laugh and move on. Now everything seemed deathly serious. I blew out a long breath and cast around for something to say.

Entrée arrived, giving us both a topic of conversation and an excuse not to talk. Boy, they can cook here. Whenever we go out we go through the pretence of deciding where to come, but we always end up at Saggio di Vino. You can taste the passion for food. Steven's much more of a foodie than me, despite the café. I like simple, old fashioned flavours and could eat the same thing every day for weeks. Steven likes variety and new tastes. We joke that I should be grateful that it's food where he indulges this enthusiasm for variety.

"Carpaccio good?"

"Mmm."

I smiled. I do like watching him enjoy himself. We have friends who say they hardly get into a restaurant before they're wanting to head home to bed. We, on the other hand, would linger till the staff are wanting to go home themselves. Dessert, cheese, port or cognac, and way too replete when we got home for anything but falling fast asleep. Before the children we'd sometimes make up for it with a fast roll through the bedclothes before getting dressed to go out. We could have done that today. It hadn't occurred to me. Maybe if we had we'd be in better moods.

It's not over yet. Try again. The owner, Lisa, came over to ask about the food, and she and Steven talked about the specialist suppliers she used. She's unique: German and strong with a gravelly voice and barking laugh. She really knows her business and is passionate about it. A role model. I made a couple of mental notes.

"She really is something!" I said as she walked away.

"Yes, great to see someone who cares so much about what they do." He reached over to pour me the last of the champagne.

"Thank you."

His comment annoyed me. Why didn't he say the same thing about my business, what I was doing? Why didn't he give me the same respect and admiration? Why didn't he take me seriously?

"Got any ideas about where you'd like to go on holiday this year?"

"You know me, anywhere with a view and a chair for me to read my book. What about skiing, though, the girls are old enough." My voice was dismissive, resentful but he didn't hear it, his face lit up. He loves the snow. "Really? Would you want to ski every day?"

I shook my head, a tiny, irritable movement. "I wouldn't have to. If we go somewhere near a field, I can go or not, or come home at lunchtime. A couple of days would be fine for me. Whatever."

He grinned. "I'll have a look at places to stay, on the Internet."

For a tiny moment I realised how much I had missed his smile; I knew all I wanted to do was connect with him. Then without warning a huge wave of anger crashed over me. I watched him load his fork with meat and chew thoughtfully, and I hated him. I took a deep breath. Was I going mad? Usually I contain my anger very well, but this was different, there was no pretending to myself that this wasn't happening. Images flashed in front of me, words whizzed through my head.

A hand touched mine. "Honey, are you okay?"

"Give me a minute." I stumbled out of my chair, over the disorienting glass topped wine cellar and into the ladies. Every one of the individually folded towels was hateful to me. I leaned against the wall feeling rolling surges flow through me. How dare he belittle what I was doing, my life! How dare he assume I would look after his children day after day, week after week with no support! How dare he think whatever he thought about the smallness of my life!

I felt wildly angry and at the same time exhilaratingly free. I was a goddess, with lightning at my finger tips. I looked up and into the mirror. For the first time I could see what people meant about Kate and me, how similar we are. With deified power sparking from my eyes I connected completely with myself. Nothing was standing in my way.

What now, though? This wasn't the mood for a candlelit supper. Not the frame of mind for sitting quietly in a restaurant. I put my hands either side of the sink and stared into my black eyes. Well, what then? I could do anything I wanted. I smiled, impish. My wrath was subsiding and now I wanted to laugh. I was strong, I was powerful, I was totally and completely me.

Who cares what he thinks or says or wants when it comes to me? I will do what I want. I will do what I know is best. I will tell him what I want him to do, for the kids, for me.

I had an image of a woman I'd seen, walking along the beach with a pram. Behind and in front of her ran a dog with a long stick. He would crouch near where she would pass, the stick in his mouth, expectant. She passed without acknowledgement. He bounded around her and crouched again. "Throw the stick!" She passed again without acknowledgement. Again and again. I felt sorry for the dog, communicating his desires so clearly and being ignored. Finally he dropped the stick and dug in the sand with frantic joy, leaping backwards in the air as his front paws pulled at the sand, two, three times, then leaving the useless stick behind him – what good was it if not thrown? – he ran on ahead of the woman heading for home.

In an instant I saw myself as that preoccupied, closed-down woman. And I didn't need to be. I saw Steven as the dog, not getting what he wanted from me. It was like waking from a dream. I knew what I wanted, I would just do it, just take it. And I would forgive Steven for not understanding me. How could he? He was just a bounding dog, looking for me to throw him a stick. We would go skiing, make him happy. And I would get on with what I wanted to do, and forget about looking for approval. Was I a mortal or a god? Today I was a god.

I went back out into the restaurant and sat down as if nothing had happened. We had main course, we had dessert, we talked about skiing, about travel. I was beginning to remember how it felt to really be attracted to my husband and to feel attractive in return. Perhaps I did have enough energy for a little bedtime fun when we got home. The waitress brought port and coffee and Steven's expression changed. "Listen, there's something I've been meaning to talk to you about."

"Yes."

"It was after the other night, when Bernard was entertaining us."

"Kate seemed impressed." I said, wryly.

He smiled at the memory. "She's a great dancer."

"And you wanted to talk to me about . . ."

"You know I always wanted to be in a band when I was younger."

"But you don't play an instrument."

"Yes I do. I played the Saxophone when I was little."

I said nothing. I hadn't known this.

"But I wouldn't play that, I'd learn something, bass guitar, it's more versatile. Well, anyway, I think it's time to do it. Start a band." The words rushed out, he was nervous.

"Sure, fine, why not." I was confused about the drama of it. My simple acceptance seemed to please him excessively.

"Really?" His grin was back, bigger than ever.

"Of course. You should do whatever you want."

He leaned up out of his chair and kissed me. "Fantastic! I love you, Tasha."

Well if that's all it took to please him! We had the best sex we'd had in years.

19

Bernard started teaching Steven bass guitar. They'd have a lesson one night after work and every spare minute Steven was plunking away, picking out the riffs and rhythms. Then he'd phone Bernard. "Is this right?" He'd nod seriously and try again. "This?" then more and more practice and Bernard was back for the next lesson.

After a few weeks Bernard started putting music with it, playing along to Steven's rhythms, matching the tune to the notes he was picking out. Suddenly it seemed to have more depth. I noticed music lying around, hand written, and there were more of the same motifs over and over again in Steven's practicing. Sometimes he played with headphones on. I realised he had begun learning proper songs, Bernard's songs.

"I didn't know Bernard was a songwriter."

"Yeah, has been for years, but never did anything with it. Lazy sod. All that talent gone to waste. Till now."

"Till now?"

"Yeah, you know, the band."

"Bernard's in your band?"

"Yeah, what'd you think? You haven't seen me practising with anyone else."

I felt a little guilty. I hadn't really taken him seriously, just felt a sympathetic fondness for his sweet little face while he concentrated on learning his notes. I hadn't expected it to go any further.

"So we thought, we just need a lead guitar. Keep it simple, just three of us. Bernard can sing, and that way we only split the pay three ways."

"Scott plays guitar," I said, absently, the thought association automatic.

"From the café? Yeah, I remember. We went to see him play that time. He was good."

"Yeah." I was slow to catch up. "Pay? What do you mean?"

"When we do gigs! Come on, Tasha, you didn't think we were just going to keep playing in our living room. I'll give Scott a call."

I went back to transcribing. With between 6 and 10 interviews most weeks now I was getting behind with the processing. I'd love to find someone to do the transcripts for me but I didn't know where to start. I was also getting behind with organising my office. There were piles of paper everywhere and Steven had left a window open a few days before, the wind had come up and things had blown all over the place. It was chaos. Maybe it was time to get Wendy back in.

A year or two back I'd had shoulder surgery – a result of overdoing the home decorating – and for six weeks I hadn't touched a thing in my office. It was tiny anyway, and the desk that filled one whole wall was covered with unopened mail, contracts, newspapers. That was one of the times I had got behind with Bernard's payments. I was behind with everything. It was completely overwhelming. I had met Wendy not long before, but my instinct told me I could not let her see the place as bad as it was.

"That's my job!" she said when I tentatively broached the question. "It's supposed to be a disaster. When do you want me to come?"

I hesitated, then named a day, and it was like a miracle. In an hour and a half all the mail was opened and processed, she had written the cheques and I had signed them - she even posted them after she left - the rubbish bin was full, the desk was empty and I had the start of the simple filing system I still use (occasionally) today.

I looked around me now. Yes, it was definitely time again. I hardly had anywhere to put my feet as I sat in the armchair with my laptop and iPod. Usually I braced them against the edge of the table, toes curled backwards to avoid knocking anything off. It gave me stomach cramps.

"Hey Babe, it's Tasha! How are you?"

"Yeah, great. You?"

"Yes, flying along, I can hardly keep up. Listen, can you fit me in for an organising session?"

"Absolutely. When do you want?"

"You know me, the sooner the better."

"Okay. I've got someone new, Susan. She's great. Unless you want me to do it in person. I'm phasing out of that side of things, but as it's you . . ."

"Really? No that's fine, I'm sure she'll be great. 10 tomorrow? Brilliant."

So Wendy didn't do hands on organising any more. I knew she was busy with speaking, things must be going really well. I felt a pang that it wouldn't be her I was working with, but I like to keep calling in favours for when it really counts.

It would be great to get the office sorted. I looked around and imagined it clean and clear, empty space on the desk, the floor walkable. The tiny room was set into the eaves of the house, off the master bedroom. Steven coveted it as an en-suite, he hated having to go downstairs to shower, but this was my space. Even when I had the café I kept all my papers here. It would be disastrous to have them downstairs where the children could get in amongst them. I took a risk now and leaned around some of the piles to open the window again. The day was still and it was getting warm up here.

I sat back in my chair and put my feet up again, adjusted the iPod earphones and started it playing.

I had developed a few different ways of working. If the sound and speech were good I could do audio editing and transcribing in parallel; if there was a lot of editing to do to the speech, usually I would do that first and transfer the mp3 to my iPod to transcribe – it made it easier to pause and continue without having to switch out of the word processor. Then if the audio editing was larger scale – one client, for example, would stop and start a lot, repeating whole paragraphs to get the words out right – then I would do the transcript from the raw audio, once again on the iPod, then use that to take out the appropriate chunks of speech. It was too risky to do that on the fly, you could end up with an audio that didn't make sense, the wrong sentences and half sentences removed. I was getting better at keeping all that in my head, but this way was simpler, more fool-proof, less exhausting, and I didn't get so explosive if I was interrupted.

Today I was working on a ten minute recording for a life coach. The only thing was, I got so excited about every client that I wanted to hire them myself. That's the reason I hardly ever go in shops. I'm impulsive, and very influenced by what is in front of me. Over the years I've suffered enough buyer's remorse that I've learned to keep myself out of temptation's way.

With the interviews I had developed a different strategy – don't say anything till I've finished with the project. That way I have time to reconsider. This guy was great, but there was something that wasn't quite a fit for me, a hint of triteness in his language. I love originality. Lucky I had followed my rule or I would have been signed up for six months' coaching!

Maybe I should think about it though, even if this wasn't the right coach for me. It would be great to have someone help me focus on a couple of specific goals.

I took a CD from the drawer and started the computer writing the files onto it. I had developed a simple format for printing the CDs with client name, title and my logo with web address – it made them look so much more professional. I was just finishing the image processing and starting the print when a blast of extreme sound shot up the stairs.

"Scott!" I slid to a stop at the bottom of the stairs, staring with surprise, then went over to hug him. There was a big amplifier in the corner of the living room and Scott held his guitar by the neck in one hand.

"Hey Tasha! This timing was perfect. Two of the guys from my band are leaving to go travelling, I was looking for something new."

"But . . . Bernard."

"I know, Bernard the jerk. But Steven asked me to give him a chance. Said he's different when he's playing music. So we'll see."

The door opened and Bernard walked in, followed by Kate. My mouth dropped open. "Hey Tasha." Bernard kissed me on the cheek; I was too surprised to squirm away.

"Kate?"

"We've been out to the beach."

"You and Bernard?"

"Yeah. What do you think? Okay if I stay and watch them play?"

The little living room was over-full with the new band and five of us watching. Erica and Greta jumped about with excitement to begin with but settled down once Bernard ushered them to the sofa where Charlotte was already curled up next to me, and asked them to sit still.

Bernard put music on a stand in front of Scott and clapped a syncopated rhythm. Scott nodded, looking so professional. Kate flicked me a look and jerked her head towards him. "He's a cutie, too. How will I choose?"

I elbowed her, intensely irritated. "You're such a slut! Why choose?"

She laughed, which annoyed me even more. I opened my mouth to have another go at her but she shushed me.

"Quiet, they're starting."

"Quiet yourself!"

The first few attempts were a bit stop and go: Steven was having trouble keeping time and made it worse by being annoyed with himself. He kept apologising until both Bernard and Scott told him angrily to chill. Then we heard the beginning of something. A few ten second sequences when there was the hint of something new. Each time it fell apart again, but there was definitely something in there. Steven went to the toilet and while he was gone Scott and Bernard carried on. The song was catchy, lyrical with a quirky rhythm. The words were simple but they told a story, took us on an emotional journey. It was good. By the end all three girls were singing along. Scott walked forward and played to each of them in turn. I had a flash forward, to concerts and fans.

20

Kate and Bernard were now an item and I couldn't figure out why it irritated me so much.

"Come on, Tasha, he's a pussycat really. He's just shy, all that bluster is just to cover it up."

"Yeah, right."

"Look, imagine what it's like for him, an almost-sports star with a reputation for losing his temper. . ."

"And punching the other team! He's lucky he didn't end up in jail."

"They were mean to him, said nasty things."

"Poor dear."

"God, you're such a hypocrite! I've seen you lose it, too, you just wouldn't have the nerve to hit anyone."

"Well, what about the pinching and brushing. I told you about that way before you met him."

"He just doesn't know how to talk to women. Can't you see how it would happen, that he'd end up looking a bit of a fool."

I began to wonder if she might be right, that I had been too hard on him. I hated to admit it, even to myself. "So you're undertaking his education? Helping him become Mr. Charm?"

"No need, really, he's safer without, or rather, I am. Add charm and I'd have some serious competition, especially now he's losing weight as well. We'll soon have him back to the fit guy I've seen in the pictures. I need to get him properly hooked by then."

"So this is a long term thing?"

"As far as I can see. Oh, I know, I don't normally have much of an attention span, but this has potential. The band, too, I can do something there."

"You? What do you mean?"

"Manager. Marketing. Do for them what I did for your interviews, only more."

"But you were looking for a job."

"Not any more. This is it, I'm taking them on full time."

"But you said never go into business with family."

"Rules are made to be broken."

"And anyway, this is just a hobby for them! What would there be for you to do?"

Her eyes fogged over. "You'd better talk to Steven."

And that was how I found out. That Steven was quitting his job.

"You've got to be kidding! Do this full time? How will we live?"

"We'll have to cut back on a few things. But your interviews are going well, we can manage."

"But you're just learning. You're not that good! Are you crazy?"

His face hardened. "Thanks for the support, Tasha, I knew I could count on it."

"But, Steven . . ."

"We're doing it, Tasha, I've already resigned."

I was flummoxed for a minute, then I rallied. "But how will I work with that racket going on? And what about Scott's café?"

"Two birds with one stone. We won't be practising here, precisely because of the café. Scott's set up a stage at the back. We'll practise there."

I sat down. It didn't make sense, any of it. I couldn't see any of it. Steven plunking bass guitar and trying to make a living out of what was still an intermittently terrible noise. Scott running the café and playing guitar at the same time - how could that work? And - I was avoiding looking at this one - me as the sole breadwinner for the family for goodness knew how long.

As Susan and I sorted my office I was deep in thought. My world was revolving and I was disoriented. Bernard and Kate. Steven unemployed. This organising session seemed like my only grip on control.

Professional Organisers sometimes find themselves as de facto counsellors, so Wendy tells me - as people shed and sort their possessions they also process parts of their lives. In the practical back and forth of "What's this?" and "Where should we put these?" and the opening up of letting someone else see the extent of my chaos, it seemed natural to let out some of what was on my mind. It was such a relief. I realised there had been no-one for me to talk to who wasn't in some way wound up in my situation.

As I got through my bewilderment at what was going on around me, I moved onto my own situation, the business - Susan immediately caught the idea of the interviews - and how I needed someone to help me.

"I'm struggling to keep up with the transcripts, and I know a professional typist would be so much faster than me."

"So why don't you find one?"

"I guess there's been too much else on my mind."

"My sister is an editor. I know she works with someone. Would you like me to get you the name?"

Amazing how easy things can be.

Steven's company let him off with only two weeks' notice. Bernard was winding down his business broking – it turns out he hadn't been successful at all, his bluster about conning people was all talk, he couldn't go through with it when it came to the point. He had a couple of businesses still on his books but after that the firm he worked for was happy for him to go.

The morning after Steven stopped his job he got up and left the house as usual, even taking his usual lunch with him, just a little more casually dressed. It turns out his mum had kept his old saxophone all this time. She sent it down from Napier and after a few odd honks and squawks he had settled into a pretty convincing rendition of "Cry me a river." He took it with him to the café, but it didn't come back in the evening like the bass did – he practised the bass at home till all hours of the night.

I kept away for nearly a week but then my curiosity overcame my pride. At 2 o'clock, before I collected the girls from school, I opened the door of the café - just a crack, to stop the bell from dinging, and slipped inside.

The stage was set against the far wall, backing onto the toilets. Bernard was sitting behind a keyboard set-up and Steven was standing to the right, looking cool and relaxed, playing a simple riff I had heard over and over at home. He had finally got it down and was looking towards the customers at the nearest tables. The place was almost full and Scott was serving. Bernard was filling in the background with morphing tunes while they waited.

They hadn't seen me. I sat down quietly at a table near the window.

"Hey, play that last one again!" one of the customers called. Several others chorused agreement.

"Scott's still serving. And he's broken a string."

"He'll catch up. Go on!"

They started to play, not too loud in the airy space, an easy, cruisey melody with a floating tune. I found my finger keeping time on the table. More customers came in, leaving the door open behind them, and a couple of tourists stopped outside to listen. After a minute they came in, too. The place had never been this busy when I owned it.

There was a menu on the table with a note at the bottom: "please order at the counter" and a more sophisticated range of choices than I had offered. Maria delivered plates to the table next to mine and opened her mouth for a surprised and happy greeting. I put my finger to my lips and pointed to Steven. I would be caught any second, but I would delay it as long as I could.

"Tasha!"

Kate swirled past my table then stopped.

"Hi."

"Good to see you, come on up. Scott, I've got your string. I got a full set, for you and Steven. We wouldn't want this happening during a gig. Look, Tasha's here, lurking in the shadows!"

Steven looked up and smiled. He looked really happy. Bernard waved "Hey Tasha." I waved back but his eyes had moved on to Kate. He was drinking her in, head on one side, like a puppy on a Christmas card.

Scott smiled, too, but waved away the bag Kate offered him. "Thread it up for me, will you, Bernard? I'll just get this order done."

To cover my embarrassment I offered to help. Scott and I always worked very naturally together, so he just mimed what was needed. "Ding the bell for Maria; it's done."

"Maria, huh? How's she doing?" I raised my eyebrows.

"Shut up." He laughed sheepishly and climbed onto the stage. He took his guitar from Bernard, checked the tuning and they started the song again. The sound was richer with Scott playing. The crowd was mesmerised.

I finished putting together the food then went to the counter and served the next customer.

Maria made the coffees and Kate served, calling occasional advice to the boys. I took orders and arranged food on plates. An hour flashed by. By three the crowd was thinning and I handed my apron back to Scott. "You need more help."

"Yeah. We've only been playing a week and it gets busier every day. Those guys at the front have become regulars."

"What do you do in the mornings?"

"Bernard and Steven practise while I do the prep. And I'm training Maria to do food."

"Going to hire more?"

He grinned. "We'll see. It could be a one week wonder."

It wasn't, though. When I had appointments Steven picked the girls up from school and brought them back to the café. Those days they always came home buzzing, humming and dancing and happy. One afternoon I had a last minute booking and dropped them in on my way home. The place was full at 3:30 in the afternoon, people sitting with soft drinks and coffees, all the chairs now turned to the stage at the back of the room. There were people leaning against the walls. Kate grinned at me, nodding around. Several people were singing along to one of Bernard's faster songs. "They're learning the words! We're getting a fan base. And I got us a gig!"

Charlotte, Erica and Greta settled into a table that had just been vacated next to the stage. Kate brought them a glass of water each and patted them on the shoulders.

There were three staff now standing behind the counter. "Hey, Sonja, your shift was over at 3."

"I know, I'm just listening."

Kate held up an A4 sheet of paper, laminated, "Café Storm rehearsal schedule" showing the times the band would be in the café. She took it to the window and stuck it next to the café hours.

"Wouldn't want to disappoint people, now we won't be here all the time."

My head was spinning. Was this happening way too fast, or was I just surprised that it was happening at all? I got caught up in a song, closing my eyes and breathing into the music. I felt great. Then Kate tapped me on the arm. "Hey, didn't you have an appointment?"

"Oh, yeah, thanks!"

I ran out, up the street to where I had parked the car. Something was different. It was all beginning to make sense.

21

This meeting was my most important so far. I'd had a call from an event organiser who had asked to meet. They wouldn't say who, but they had a big time author who didn't want to do a formal speech but might be willing to be interviewed. So the organiser was interviewing me.

I had dressed up, camel-coloured suit and leather clutch purse containing business cards and a sheet of testimonials. There was a fine balance between too much personality and too little. It was true that the interviewee had to be the focus, but I needed to be the foil. "Don't talk too much," I told myself, "but let them know who you are."

I took the discrete little lift up to a small suite of offices in Hereford St. The reception area was tiny but there were large original oil paintings on each side wall and the window behind the receptionist gave a wide view over the river with the park in the distance. The company name stood out above the window in three dimensional pewter letters, sans serif. It wasn't the name I remembered on the phone.

The reception coffee table held current issues of Vogue from three different countries and the receptionist looked like she had materialised out of one of them. I'd so love to be able to do makeup like that, but now wasn't the time for fashion tips.

"Ms Stuart. Mr Leman is waiting, please follow me."

Mr Leman? That wasn't the name. There wasn't time to ask, it was only two steps to the left hand office. The receptionist preceded me then stepped back to let me pass.

"Ms Stuart, Tasha, a pleasure. I'm Kent Leman, literary agent."

"Mr Leman, I was expecting to see Mr Sutton."

"Yes . . . I asked him to set up this appointment, I wanted to discuss the need for discretion in person before you were told in detail about what we are looking for."

"You want an in-person interview."

"Yes."

"For a client."

"Yes."

"Someone important."

"Yes."

"So you don't want anyone to know about it beforehand, to know they are coming. You want me to keep it a secret. You want to make sure I am capable of keeping it a secret."

"Partly. There is more to it than this, however." He pulled the corner of his lower lip between his teeth and chewed it. "We require secrecy about who the subject is and where the interview is held until the interview is released. I am sure you will be able to satisfy this requirement with the right inducement.

"More important is the sympathy required to create the right impression. What I need to ascertain from you today is that you are capable of this sympathy. You say on your website that you bring out the best in your clients, their passion. Is this true?"

"Yes. I believe everyone does what they do because they have a passion for it, or began with a passion for it. I help them get in touch with this during the interview and communicate it. The emotion is contagious. The audience feels with the person being interviewed, learns to trust them."

"I see."

There was a long pause. Mr Leman steepled his fingers and closed his eyes. I waited, breath held. Finally his upper lip twitched briefly and he inhaled audibly through his nose.

"We are taking a calculated gamble with you. I have listened to the interviews you have on your site so far, and there is something unique here. A difference of approach, of assumption. I sum it up by saying that it appears your interview subjects are your market, not the audience of the interview. They are entertaining, but they are not entertainment. Your subjects indeed come across very sympathetically. You are aiming at portraying them well, not creating spectacle. There are more experienced interviewers, higher profile, people who would handle this interview well."

"Yes."

"With you, however, I think we can communicate the message as we desire to; communicate the persona in a way that will satisfy. We have a book that requires some introduction, from someone who has lived an unusual life, a controversial life, who is eager to be understood and to experience a degree of acceptance from the world which is at this point uncertain. You can help."

"Yes, I'm sure . . ."

"There is just one more critical question."

"Yes . . ?" I leaned forward on my seat. The man was mesmerising.

"Do you, would you say, have an unconquerable prejudice against the perpetrators of white collar crime?"

22

Steven was animated at dinner. Rehearsals were going well and Kate had lined up a series of modest gigs for them to play. Just as well he was so excited, he didn't notice my preoccupation.

"Schools and old people's homes to start with. Kate says we need hours on the stage. The café is good, the audience makes us focus for our practice, but a real gig, entrance, exit, the shape of the play list, we need experience in this, too, if we're going to make the big time."

"Uh huh," I agreed.

"We're working on a few covers. Bernard's stuff is great but we need more variety if the regulars are going to keep interested. Scott's doing great in the café, too, hired a new waitress this afternoon, Kate's orders. She's a tyrant but she'll get us where we're going."

"Sure."

"Shame we didn't get this started while you had the café, although I guess it wouldn't have been as much your style as it is Scott's. And he says it plays hell with the ordering, he never knows from one day to the next what the crowd will be and what they'll want, and he's lost focus on that a bit, with having so much fun playing and now we'll be there some of the time and not others he's not sure how that will affect business and Tasha are you listening to me at all?"

"Mm hmm."

"Then this will be time to tell you that if you're okay with it, Kate has also booked us a gig at a strip joint for Saturday night."

"Mm hmm."

"And if that works out, she's thinking about getting us a regular slot there. Are you okay with me being out most weekends? It'll mean some money coming in, but, well, I wasn't sure whether you'd mind."

"Money coming in?" He had got my attention at last. "From the band?"

"Yeah."

"That's great! Well done! Wow!" It had never occurred to me that they might really make it work, but I didn't want to say this to him now.

"And you're okay with where it's coming from?"

I also didn't want to admit I hadn't been listening. "Sure, fine," I said, vaguely. My dilemma was pulling me back in. I replayed Kent's words again and again. I had promised not to discuss it with anyone; it was taking all my will power to keep my mouth shut about something so mind-boggling and it was the biggest decision of my admittedly short career. There were so many angles to think about. Actually, there were only two major ones: could I resolve my moral questions about the interview, and if not, would I do it anyway?

I sat with Wendy over coffee and tried to focus on her question: "What did I want next?" She does this to me once in a while. I have tried turning the tables on her, asking what her next plans are, but it always turns out she has already brainstormed, come up with a wildly ambitious list, written a blog about it and achieved two of them the week before.

"Come on, you know it will help. Think."

I stared down at the piece of paper in front of me, my old list:

> Interview a chef
>
> Do a live interview
>
> Interview someone famous
>
> Get a book project

"Isn't this enough?"

"You've done it all, or near enough. How's Arthur's book going, by the way? You've started?"

Arthur was someone we both knew from National Speakers. Like so many others, he'd always wanted to write a book, but never found time.

"Yeah, good." I smiled as my mind wandered again, into the delights of working with someone who really knew their stuff. It was hard to tell where the genius came from, it seemed so easy. I asked a few questions, he had the answers instantly. The questions were easy, the answers were easy, but without the questions the answers didn't exist. The structure was simple when you looked at the topic in overview, then the detail was easy, piece by piece as I worked from my notes with the questions prepared. Then the transcript was easy, and Arthur said editing the transcript into literate prose was easy, too. "Really good. We'll be done in a few weeks."

"And does he have a publisher? Or an agent?"

Automatically my mood fell. The book would be great, but Arthur was not confident about getting it published. We were doing it on a profit share basis, and I was systematically suppressing my pessimism about ever getting paid. "Not yet. I . . . Hold on!" The book was great, but we didn't have a publisher. I sort of felt that was Arthur's responsibility. I certainly didn't know where to start with that aspect so I'd brushed his despondence aside, told him I knew he could do it. But maybe . . . maybe now I knew a literary agent, there was something I could contribute after all. It would help if I got Kent in the mood for listening by doing him a favour.

"Yes? Something you want to share?"

"No, but, Wendy, you're a genius!"

"You have no idea."

23

Steven was evasive that evening about why I needed to pick up the girls from school. "I said, we were checking out the venue for Saturday."

"And they couldn't come with you? I had plans I had to change."

"No, sorry Hon, they couldn't." He looked at me sideways and turned away when I opened my mouth to ask some more. "Sometimes it will work out that way. We agreed to compromise, didn't we?"

"Just give me more notice next time, if you can. Or maybe I'll ask Kate for a copy of your schedule."

"No, need," he said, quickly. "I'll let you know."

He was making smoked salmon with cucumber and cream, one of my favourites. Yesterday had been tarragon chicken, which he also knows I'm a sucker for.

"I'm feeling spoiled."

"Always the best for you, Darling." He wrapped his arms around me, holding his sticky hands out from my body in fists.

"So was it good?"

"What?"

"The venue? Good acoustics, décor?"

"You know I never think about the décor. I hardly looked."

105

And for some reason, he had to turn away to hide a smirk.

Steven had given the girls dinner earlier and they were curled up in front of a movie.

"Let's take this upstairs."

"Where to? My office?"

He lead me through the bedroom and onto the tiny balcony, where he had rigged up a little table hanging off the balustrade. He lit a candle lantern and we pulled up barstools and looked out at the evening sky. He reached down and pulled a bottle of champagne out of an ice bucket.

"We're celebrating?"

"Our first paid gig."

"Yeah. Wow."

"I've missed you, Tasha, I haven't been the best husband for a while now. But now I'm doing what I love, I feel like I've come back to myself. It's like opening up the house again after being away. Like coming home. I guess I'm also remembering I love you."

"Aw!" I felt a tear in the corner of my eye.

"The idea of being able to support my family doing something I love is fantastic!"

"Sure. But you shouldn't have to do it alone. In fact, I have something to celebrate, too. I got an interview job. A big one. It means travelling away, so I've been hesitating. But I want to contribute financially, too, and . . ." Shut up, Tasha! I was thinking aloud, and with the secret I had to keep that was dangerous. "Here's to success! For both of us."

Steven leaned in and kissed me. We clinked glasses and I inhaled the new-bread aroma, fizz sprinkling my nose. If anything relaxes my inhibitions, it's champagne. Oh well. Perhaps if I focused on physical abandon I could still keep my mouth shut.

The salmon is a dish that doesn't take long to eat, so we retired to bed with the rest of the bottle. I knew the movie well enough from repeated viewings with the girls that I could follow progress from the bursts of loud music. "We have about 35 minutes till it's finished."

Steven rolled me over, wrapping me in the sheet so my arms were pinned to my sides. "A bit of a rush, but we should be okay as long as you don't distract me."

TASHA STUART INTERVIEWS . . .

24

I was on the plane and very nervous, sitting next to Kent Leman. 'Till the last minute they hadn't given me the name of my subject and even when they did, it meant nothing to me. The plane would take us to Nelson and we would meet the guy at a hotel near the airport. I had an advance copy of the book in my hand. It was open, but my efforts to take in any content of significance were not going well. My stomach was sinking for so many reasons, and it just seemed to keep going down and down. There must be some kind of rotation system going on down there; again and again I felt the plunge in my belly. I didn't think I could throw up again. This guy was a criminal; would there be guns? I have only seen guns in movies, and until "Die Hard" I closed my eyes whenever I saw them even there. The machine gun wielding guards in Eastern Europe when I was travelling I had managed to block out by quoting myself statistics, but here, at this meeting, if they wanted to shoot someone it would just as likely be me.

And then, this was a huge interview for me. I was nervous enough about the ten minute promotions I did at home; I hadn't been able to prepare at all, so all my pre-patter about things going well, the unconscious mind doing the work, were out the window. All that, and I don't much like flying. If I had to choose, I wondered idly, would I rather crash or be shot? Surprisingly I didn't find the speculation comforting.

"The seatbelt sign has now been turned on. Please prepare for landing." No comfort, either, in the fact that the flight was so short it had hardly been turned off. We were still only half way there, but every second ticked closer to my ravenous fear.

We were met by the scariest guy I've ever been close to, built to intimidate, and he probably practised in the mirror as well. He handed us over to a black suited driver who took us out to the waiting car and ushered us into the back seat. For 30 seconds I expected the engine to start, but nothing happened. The driver started drumming his fingers nervously on the wheel.

"Kent . . ." I began, but he put a finger to his lips. We must be waiting for the Scary Guy. I looked at my watch. Ten minutes ticked by, and then there was a noise at the back of the car, the boot opening and I felt a backward pull as something heavy was put inside. There was another long pause. I turned my head to look out the back of the car, but Kent put a hand on my arm and I faced forward again.

Scary Guy got into the front passenger seat, jerking his head to indicate we should pull out. The ride was smooth, so I barely noticed how fast the car accelerated.

"Change of plan," Scary Guy muttered when we were out of the airport. Beads of sweat were gathering along his shaved hairline. "We're going to the house. Drive along the motorway and stop. The chopper will pick us up." The driver looked at him in surprise.

"Everything all right?" Kent leaned forward towards him.

"Everything's fine." The man's tone invited no further questions.

I've never been in a helicopter before. I've always thought it would be fun but having Scary Guy bundle me into my seat took the edge off my pleasure. The view was spectacular as we took off from Nelson, out to sea and back over the rolling hills behind the town. It was windy. We flew West towards the complex folds of the Takaka Hill catching glimpses of the road as we flew up. The wind knocked us from side to side, often feeling like a solid physical blow. At one point there was a sideways lurch combined with a fall which took us straight towards a bush-covered hillside. Kent and I exchanged terrified glances. I couldn't hear anything over the sound of the engine and rotors but I can read lips if the content is simple and the Scary Guy had his face towards me. He was swearing. He gestured a wide circle and the pilot nodded, turning back in a wide arc the way we had come and taking us out to sea. It looked like we were taking the long route.

We landed in a field next to a country tennis court. The hill rose steeply behind us. "We'll have to wait here for transport. We can't land at the house in this wind."

Kent moved away from the helicopter and sat down on a sloping area of grass. I almost expected him to take out a handkerchief to sit on. "Come over here, my dear. Perhaps you might do some more reading. I noticed your mind wasn't completely focused on the plane."

Why not? I took the book from my shoulder bag and opened at the first page again. I had hardly taken anything in. This time, however, even with the wind buffeting and looking up at every passing car, I was quickly engrossed. I was entering a foreign world, seeing something of an intelligent, sensitive mind. I was several chapters in before I began to make sense of certain euphemistic phrases which appeared repeatedly, embedded in urbane dialogue. Here was a businessman – referred to simply as "Boss" in the reported conversations, narration in the first person, the W.D. Hero of the front cover – who employed well developed logic in his decision making, restraint in responding to errors, with a fondness for the people he employed. The other side of what was happening was obscured under eloquence and allusion, like a nose blown with a silk handkerchief.

The voice of the author got in. I liked this person, I could relate to him. And when I began to suspect what was going on underneath, I felt sick, like it had become a part of me. White collar crime, Kent had said. Was that all?

A four wheel drive pulled up and I put the book away. Scary Guy caught sight of it and smiled. "The book's pretty good, huh? We're all very proud."

Pride? What sort of pride would a tattoo-ridden, hairy-armed thug understand? Wow, I must be nervous, I normally keep my inner bigot under control.

"I'm Ham, by the way."

I tentatively held out my hand. His handshake was considerately gentle. "Hi, Ham. I'm Tasha."

"Short for Hamlet," he elaborated, and this time I could hear the pride in his voice. "Yeah, I know, Tasha Stuart. I heard your interview with that chef guy. It was great."

I smiled. A warm feeling glowed in my chest, surprising under the circumstances. He held out his arm towards the vehicle and I climbed into the back seat, Kent following behind.

The road up the hill was narrow, windy, bumpy, with a couple of streams to cross and gates to open and close. A couple of times we passed cyclists. "Boss won't like that," Ham murmured. It was only 8 or 10 kilometres but it took the best part of half an hour. Finally we reached another gate and from there the short drive was groomed and clean. As the vehicle pulled up beside the house, facing out towards a steep drop over a retaining wall, I felt like I was on the top of the world.

The view was straight out over farmed valleys to the sea. The road was visible in several places. I thought I caught sight of a cycle helmet flashing briefly in the sun. No-one would be able to get up here without being seen. I looked towards the house. From this side it was like a fortress, blank walls with only small glazed slits for observation.

Ham opened my door and held out his arm. "Come on, I'll take you inside. The Boss is waiting to meet you."

TASHA STUART INTERVIEWS . . .

25

It turned out The Boss was not waiting to meet me.

"Migraine," said Ham, shortly. "Boss hates the wind."

As he said this I became aware of the intense howling on the other side of the thick walls. It rose and fell like a Wagnerian opera. It didn't bother me, particularly – in fact it seemed very consistent with the mood of my experience.

"You won't be able to do the interview today, not until the wind dies down. There's recovery time, too. So not before tomorrow afternoon."

"But my flight . . ." I looked at Kent. I had already been a little concerned about making it back in time for 5:30.

"We can change your flight, of course. Will it be terribly inconvenient for you to stay until tomorrow?"

My chest constricted. Every instinct said to refuse. But then Ham smiled encouragingly. "I can show you to a guest room, you can freshen up."

"Okay," I said. Might as well make the best of it. I wasn't sure what the response would be if I said no, and I had no chance of making it back to Nelson against their wishes. Ham seemed okay and Kent was a gentleman, I was sure. I watched Ham walk over to a cupboard, take something from inside his jacket and put it away. As he closed the cupboard I glimpsed complex metal shapes. Were they guns? Ham closed the door again and locked it, putting the key in his pocket.

"Here. You can have the gold suite."

I followed him through interior corridors with a series of closed doors on one side, blank wall on the other. This part of the house must be built back into the hill. He took another key from his pocket and unlocked a double door, throwing it wide open to reveal an opulent room – gold, in fact, in every direction. At the end of the room was a wall of glass overlooking the valley to the west. At the far right I could just see the sea. The range of hills on the far side of the valley seemed to go on forever, but I knew the West Coast was not many miles away. Optical illusion. The mind playing tricks.

"Make yourself at home. There's an internal phone if you want anything. Drinks in the fridge. Dinner will be at 6. I'll come and get you."

"Kent?"

"He'll be at dinner. You'll be safer here."

I frowned, wondering what he meant, but he was turning away, closing the door.

"Oh, by the way, if you're calling home, best to watch what you say. For everyone's sake." The door clicked closed then clicked again. After a moment I tried the handle. It was locked.

I looked around. It was like a hotel room, one of those pictures you see of Luxury in the Orient in magazine advertisements. There was a huge, wall-hung television. I turned it on for a minute, cartoons. I flipped the remote:

news, a politician had been kidnapped. From Nelson airport – that was a coincidence, but otherwise local politics bore me. I wandered aimlessly into the bathroom, slid my eyes over gold and white towels stacked on marble, gold taps over the bath and basin.

A bath! That was what I needed. I took a reflexive visual sweep of the room for cameras, then figured, what the hell? I needed to unwind, badly, or I might explode.

Wrapped in a huge towel with another draped over the pillow for my wet hair, I opened the book. It was 2 p.m. I had four hours to read before dinner. Almost immediately I closed it again. I was hungry and I should call Steven. I had put it off.

What would I say? Would he hear the fear in my voice, say something that would give us away? Tone down the melodrama, Tasha, nobody's threatening you, and you knew you were getting into unfamiliar territory. What's the difference between being here for an hour and staying the night? Reasonable question, and I didn't have a logical answer. But there definitely was a difference.

Really it was pretty simple. "Steven, my interview subject has a migraine and can't do it today. I'm going to stay overnight and see if he's better tomorrow. Will you be okay with the girls?"

"Sure. You okay?"

"I'm fine." No, no I'm not! Save me!

"Okay, we'll see you tomorrow. We'll miss you."

"Me too."

I wanted to scream as he hung up before me. Didn't he know I needed him? I told myself to get a grip. Lie down. Read. It was a credit to the story that within minutes I had forgotten where I was.

Would it be rude to read at dinner? I decided it would be, and besides, I would need something to do if I couldn't sleep tonight. The wind was quieter in my room, but it was still blowing wild in the upstairs living space. It was just Kent, Ham and me at dinner. Ham was serving and I realised as he talked us through the dishes he had also cooked. The flutter of his eyelashes as I complimented him was almost pretty, especially when contrasted with the tattoos showing through his stubbly hair.

"The Boss still suffering?" I asked with concern. I felt like I knew him well now, and I felt sympathy. "I've had a couple of migraines myself, so I know what it's like. Does he take anything for them?"

Kent and Ham exchanged a look I didn't understand. Ham shook his head gently then turned back to me, but without catching my eye.

"Yeah, there's something. But when the wind's up like this there's nothing much that makes a difference. Camomile tea and a dark room and wait till it's over."

"This can't be the best place to live then," I said, cautiously.

"For some things it is and some things it isn't. What do you think of the sauté potatoes?"

Thinking it best to go with the change of subject I complimented the vegetables heartily. And they were terrific. I realised that I was beginning to feel bizarrely at home.

26

I finished The Boss's book, with its thrilling finale, and lay back on the pillows reliving it. It had a sense of unreality, like I was reading fiction. Portrayed in subtle tints of light and dark, the characters created logic within the murky ambiguity. Much like it is possible to watch violence in film once you sympathise with the protagonist, despise the antagonist and understand the situation to be constrained to one possible outcome, I could understand and approve actions which were well outside my moral code. I could even see a wild courage to acts which were unthinkable, and inevitable.

And this was the person I would interview tomorrow. The purpose of my visit had gone from my mind as I read, but now I needed to think about how the recording would go. What was the purpose of it? Why was I here? Everything that would excuse The Boss's actions to the world were here in the book. People had only to read it, and I was sure they would feel as I did.

I remembered back to the end of my first meeting with Kent. "It's the book's introduction to the world, for those with a short attention span. We are sure you are the right person for the job. Just bring the same sympathy to this interview as you have to the others."

That had been my dilemma, of course. Ought I to feel sympathy for someone who had committed crimes? And in retrospect, had they really been crimes? Everything was so vague, so veiled. I thought I knew what I was reading, but had anything definite been said?

Well, I had made my choice, said yes to the opportunity, and after reading his book I was sure that that expedient decision had been right. Thank goodness! What would I have done, here, in this position, if I decided now I shouldn't do it? This would be much easier.

I closed my eyes, replaying scenes in my mind. I hadn't expected to sleep but when the sound of the helicopter woke me I found myself in a fresh new day.

The wind was down and The Boss was well enough this morning for a brief pre-interview. I had told Kent it was a good idea, likely to make the full interview later go smoothly. I ran my hands over my light top. I had washed it out the night before and it really needed ironing. Maybe I should have asked, but it was too late now.

I was nervous, sick nervous. Any minute now I would meet him. What would he be like? The book covered events over the last four or five years, finishing at most six months before. I had the impression he might be youngish, maybe only 30 or 35, although my preconceptions of criminal bosses made a much older mental picture.

"What does the W.D. stand for?" I whispered to Kent. "What should I call him?"

Again the glance between Kent and Ham. I noticed Ham's jacket back on and strained to see whether there were any suspicious bulges underneath it.

"The Boss will tell you. You'll be fine." Kent squeezed my hand, and for a moment I wondered who he was trying to reassure.

The door opened. In walked a beautiful but pale-looking teenage girl, white blonde hair hanging straight down either side of her face. She walked up to me, holding out a slight, long-fingered hand. "Hi. You're Tasha. I'm Winnie. Winifred Domenica Hero. There's more to this story than you might have been lead to believe."

TASHA STUART INTERVIEWS . . .

27

I held her hand, staring into her face. Light blue veins surrounded her snow-blue eyes. My mind flashed back over the book and found nothing to directly contradict her.

"How did this happen?"

She smiled slightly, and gave a quiet laugh. "That's a complicated story. I'm going to tell it to you, and I want you to help me tell it to the world. I want you to help me convince the world I'm human." She gestured towards a sofa. I stumbled as I turned. Ham caught me and as I straightened I looked up into his face. He nodded, and gave me a small, sad smile.

"Dad's been running this business for fifty years. Actually he's a genius, the way he looks at systems and finds the flaws. He wouldn't define what he does as crime, more like seeing loopholes and mining them, much like you would find a seam of gold and dig it out. From the outside it can be hardly visible, while on the inside . . . well, I don't know how to continue the metaphor, but you get my meaning."

"I'm not sure, explain again." We made eye contact for a moment, until I broke away.

"But I haven't answered your question, and it's important. Dad ran a large team of people, closely managing each of them individually. I'm his youngest child by many years; an old man's last fling. My older brothers and sisters moved away. Once they were adults they didn't want to get caught up in what was happening, although they're happy enough to turn a blind eye when they need money. My father's first wife – only wife, actually, he never married my mother – is a shrewd woman, the definitive successful gambler. She knew when to cash in her chips and walk away. At the first sign of trouble she left him. He was arrested and tried for fraud 20 years ago. It didn't stick but when he got back home she was gone. He used to joke she left with only a suitcase. But it's amazing how many share certificates and diamonds a suitcase can hold. She didn't bother packing clothes."

"Used to? I thought your father was still alive."

Her eyes dulled, as if she wasn't inside them any more. "Sort of. Occasionally. He has Alzheimer's. He's in a place where they take very good care of him."

I waited, but she was deep in thought. "I still don't understand."

A shadow crossed her face. Ham stepped forward with his hand out. "No, it's okay," she said, eyes still on me. He hovered for a moment then stepped back towards the door where he had been standing. "When the disease began, the first thing we noticed was that he started making mistakes. I think we both realised at the same time that something was happening. His plans were always complex and delicate. He would share them with me. My half brothers and sisters didn't have much aptitude for it, but I did, I'm a natural, I've been learning at his knee since I was four." She smiled a Halloween smile. I leaned a little further back in my chair.

"For a while he knew enough that we could hide his condition between us. We pretended he had a voice impairment and needed me to talk for him. We'd pretend to confer, then I'd give orders. But really I was making the decisions. I was 12." Laser-like pride shone from her eyes, but a moment later tears formed. "That was okay for a couple of years, but then he began to lose it to an extent it was hard to hide. He needed care, discrete care, completely away from people who would triumph in his weakness. Father had fewer scruples than I, he grew up tougher. I have always been adored." She turned away, brought a hand to her cheek momentarily then lowered it. "I couldn't let people know. I needed to hide him away. I invented business interests in another city which he was 'travelling to take care of' – I would take time with decisions, pretend they were still coming from him, and gradually increased my 'areas of authority'. After a while everyone got used to taking orders from me. The only one who has known the truth all along is Ham. And now Kent. And you. It's delicate information. There are still projects in progress . . . I'll be seventeen next month. That alters my level of legal risk. I'm not as clever as my father." Ham cleared his throat and she turned towards him. "I'm not, I know it." She turned back to me. "I'm not always so certain of staying on the right side of the law." She looked down at her hands. "And . . . And I don't have his courage. I need to find a way out."

There was a long silence. Kent, Ham and I watched her closely, anticipating her next words.

She wiped a hand over her left cheek and eye, then looked up at me. "I need to find a way out, and I think it's you."

We talked through what she wanted to say in the interview, the essential points she wanted to communicate. The timing needed to be precise, releasing the recording to the media at the moment when the book was generating maximum curiosity, and coinciding with the completion of her final projects. She was certain she could handle things to coordinate the two. It was up to Kent to manage the book marketing and then create the appropriate splash with our tape.

My standard questions were undergoing adaptation on the fly. "What is the most exciting benefit your clients get from working with you?" just didn't seem appropriate under the circumstances.

"I'll talk about the book, that it was a preamble to dismantling our organisation. You can't just walk away and let things fall, it has to be carefully done, or it would expose the weaknesses we have found in global organisations, cause panic and collapse. I have to be responsible. There is a lot of money involved, and other people, personalities who are better, very much better, not left to their own judgement of how best to protect their own interests.

"My priority is to secure the family fortune and take apart the business. We are a long way down that path. But the final phase of it requires this public declaration, and it's critical, now I'm nearly seventeen, that no possible crime can be seen to be committed. Father's not been competent to be considered responsible for my actions for a long time. I have doctors' letters to back that up. But now . . . the game is different. I have no intention of risking prison. I want a quiet life. I want freedom. And I want to keep the money I've earned – I'm accustomed to luxury. And even after everything, a certain amount of attention to security is required."

I stared out the window for a minute, trying to translate this into structure and content and questions, but another question was haunting me. "Okay, that's clear, I'll work up a list of questions for you to look over. Can I ask one other thing?"

"Sure."

"What about your mother? Where does she come into this?"

For a moment I saw deep hurt, crazed betrayal cross her face. Her fingers curled into claws. Ham stepped between us.

"For God's sake, Ham, get back. I'm not a child any more. You don't need to protect her from me. I have myself well under control." She turned back to me, nose twitching, and spoke slowly, as if addressing a foreigner. "I will write you a list of questions, you will work from those. Be ready at 2."

It was my simplest interview ever. Ham made sure I understood I was to ask only the questions on the list. Winnie was fluent, polished, hardly a hesitation in her speech. The direction surprised me a little, there was obviously more to it than she had told me thus far. I had a dim sense of being part of a larger puzzle, and of not being able to see the other pieces. Like a pawn with a blindfold, I was useful, and I didn't need to know how.

She stood up and held out her hand with a polite, restrained smile. "When will you have the finished files?"

"Tomorrow. There's hardly any editing to do."

"And can you drop them off at Leman's? In person?"

"Yes."

"Okay. It's important that once I have given approval of the product that you destroy all other copies and files. Fine?"

"Yes."

"Ham, you'll cover my other requirements before you let her go."

Ham nodded. As she turned away I saw an expression of fond devotion cross his face. He took me by the arm and lead me towards the helicopter, motioning Kent to stay away. The pilot was not there, and the engine was off. Ham all but lifted me into the back seat.

"Okay. Listen carefully. This is important. She told you some stuff, I'm not sure why, that no-one else knows. The Boss doesn't do anything arbitrarily, so there'll be a reason for it, but I don't know what it is. It is VERY important that you say nothing of this to anyone. If you're not sure what you can say, say nothing. Once the interview is public, you can talk about that, but stick to that and nothing else. Got it?"

Keeping my mouth shut. My favourite sport! At least I was getting better at it. And it seemed important. I nodded.

"Also no-one knows where she lives. It was a last minute change that made it necessary to bring you here, and she's not happy about it. It was my fault. I made a mistake . . . Anyway, whatever . . . people may try to get you to say. Make something up. There is danger otherwise. Got it?"

I nodded again. There was a pause as Ham considered what he was about to say. "Listen, about her mother . . . she left when The Boss was seven. Broke her heart. She never talks about it. Go easy on her and don't ask again?"

I didn't need his warning; I nodded once more. He hugged me, tight. That was a surprise. "Take care of yourself. You're okay." He got out of the helicopter.

"You're not coming?"

He gestured to Kent and the pilot who were standing near the house.

He smiled fondly. "I've done my job with you. You're safe."

I watched him walk away without a backward glance and felt very strangely sad.

28

I geared myself up for the exhilaration of the helicopter flight but I couldn't feel it. I found myself looking away into the distance, registering nothing, lost in replaying images and words in my mind.

Kent handled everything at the airport, checked us both in for the flight and ushered me down the gangway onto the plane. I took the window seat he gallantly offered without remembering to thank him. The engines started, the plane took off and I began to shake. I leaned forward in my seat, bringing my face as close as possible to my knees and began to cry.

After a minute I felt a comforting hand on my back. The worst of the episode was over; I sat up.

"Thanks, Kent. I don't know what . . ."

"You've been very brave. Very brave. I'm sorry I put you in that position. You did marvellously."

"Really? I was completely out of my depth. Are all your clients like that?"

"There's usually a degree of eccentricity. We're quite a specialised service."

"Specialised how, exactly?"

"Well . . ." he looked at me discerningly. "I suppose I do owe you a certain amount, and you're under a promise of secrecy. I think of us as decorators. Whitewash, mostly. We give people a new face, a new coat of paint. When people want to change direction they come to us."

I thought this over for a moment. "When they want to change direction, and also when they want to appear to have changed direction?"

He bowed his head slightly.

"And which is it in this case?"

He pursed his lips and I thought for a moment he would not answer. "In this case, my dear, I am not entirely sure. Ah, drinks! Will you have an orange juice?"

"Thanks." I concentrated on opening the foil top without spilling the contents. It's a unique feeling, the flat lipped pottle uncomfortable against the top lip. The sugar felt good. "I think I might be in shock."

"You might be. Indulge yourself. Cry some more, if you like."

I shook my head, staring out the window as the clouds swirled around us. There was so much still to absorb.

A flight attendant came through with a small child offering sweets. I took one, then remembered I hate them and put it in my bag. I took a deep breath and sighed. After everything that had happened, it seemed silly to be nervous about broaching this new subject with Kent; it was now or never, however.

"There's something else I wanted to ask you, and I know I'm taking a liberty."

"Well?"

"You know I do book work with my interviews as well?"

"Yes."

"Well I'm just finishing a book draft with a business coach here in town. I wondered if you would take a look at it. The content is interesting and practical, and the subject is also a professional speaker. I hoped you might consider acting as agent."

"I see. And do you think it fits with our market niche? Given what I told you just now?"

"Well, no, I guess not."

"Let me see it. I suspect we won't be able to take it, but I might be able to pass it on to someone suitable."

"You know other agents?"

"Of course, my dear. And they often pass projects on to me. Afraid to play with fire, most people." The smile which followed this statement was private, not meant for me. He dropped his eyes to the in-flight magazine and smirked to himself all the way back home.

TASHA STUART INTERVIEWS . . .

29

I walked in the door and dropped my bag on the kitchen table. Steven looked up from peeling vegetables at the sink. He held aside his wet hands and leaned his cheek out to be kissed.

"Charlotte, Erica, Greta, Mum's home!"

They came running through. I held out my arms and was almost knocked over. I closed my eyes and squeezed them tight. "I missed you all."

"Mum, Mum, look!" My eyes opened.

"Erica, what's this?"

"Erica's got chicken pox!"

Erica half smiled then burst into tears.

"Steven?"

"She came out in spots yesterday. She's pretty miserable, aren't you, Babe?"

"Come on, Honey, back to bed." I persuaded the others to find something else to do and lead Erica through to the bedroom. She climbed into bed and I pulled the covers over her.

"How is it?"

"It itches, and I feel sad all the time."

"Can I bring you something? Something to eat? A drink?"

"Can I have some lemonade?"

"Sure. I'll go to the supermarket. Anything else?"

"No, but I'm bored."

"Do you have a book?"

"I can't concentrate."

"Shall I find the portable DVD player? You can watch a movie." Her eyes lit up. I had a rare moment of knowing I was getting something right.

"You wait here, Honey, I'll be back soon."

I found the DVD player and set her up, then took my wallet and drove down to the supermarket. I ran over the next few days in my mind. She would be contagious for at least a week, and that meant she couldn't go to school, or to the café with Steven, and no clients over for interviews, at least until she was feeling a lot better.

When I got back Steven was just putting dinner in the oven.

"How are we going to handle this?"

He shrugged. "I don't know. It's really bad timing. We have gigs almost every day – Kate's got obsessed with getting us as much stage time as possible – I can't let the guys down." He hesitated, nervous. "What about you?"

I rubbed the inside corner of my eye and sank down onto a kitchen chair. After the day I'd had I was too tired to think, really. I considered the idea of taking a few days off, sitting with Erica, looking after her, giving her all the attention I'd wished my mum had given me. From here that looked pretty great. I'd have to let go of a couple of interviews, reschedule them for a week or so, and I had Winnie's interview to process and some others to complete, but I could do that in the quiet times. I could even sit in Erica's room and do it, so I'd be there if she needed me. Actually it looked pretty great.

"Okay, I can do it. I'll cancel the appointments I have so I can be here for the rest of the week."

Steven put his arms around me. "Thanks, Honey. Hey, how contagious is chicken pox?"

"Very. I expect to see Greta and Charlotte with it in a couple of weeks."

"Should we try to keep them away?"

"No point. It's most contagious before the spots show."

"Ah."

"What?"

"Well, I haven't had it. Do you think there's a chance I'll get it, too?"

A chance? I'd say about 100%. Maybe I'd better put things on hold for a bit longer.

Steven, Greta and Charlotte all started showing spots within about 12 hours of each other. Actually that worked out fine, Steven was there with them while they were off school and although he was miserable, Greta was cheerful and could deliver drinks and other necessities to the other two for a few hours at a time. She loved having the responsibility. The only thing was finding somewhere quiet I could meet and interview clients. I needed somewhere pretty soundproof and, if at all possible, free.

I had delivered Arthur's book to Kent with the Winnie files and was wondering when I could reasonably follow up.

Steven hated missing rehearsals and gigs but Bernard had rigged up recordings of his bass line so they were doing okay. A friend was picking up Erica and bringing her home, so actually there wasn't too much for me to do. And the big upside was I hadn't seen Bernard for almost a month.

"He hasn't had it either, he's keeping clear," Steven explained. "But I thought you guys were getting along fine now."

"Yeah, still . . ."

Maybe I could phone Kent today. It wouldn't take him long to read the first couple of pages if he hadn't already. I was sure he wouldn't mind.

"Tasha, are you listening?"

I looked down at Steven and was shocked to see tears in his eyes. "Honey?"

"You weren't listening and I'm so lonely and I feel terrible and it's not fair."

I put my hand on his head. He was burning hot. Reluctantly I put aside the idea of calling Kent and went to get Steven a cold cloth and some paracetamol. "Maybe you should come downstairs where I can keep an eye on you better."

"Then you'll go up to your office and I'll be alone again. I wish Greta was still home."

Greta and Charlotte had been back at school for a couple of days; Steven seemed much sicker than they had been. This was way out of character for him, to complain. He would often take days off when he was working his salary job, with a cold, or 'flu' but usually he just tucked himself away with a book and a box of tissues and re-emerged when he was better. He was never dependent and tearful like this.

"Maybe I should call the doctor," I said, slowly.

The receptionist was brusque. "He's been sick how long?"

"Two weeks."

"He should have been in at the start."

"But the girls were fine, you said I didn't have to bring Erica in."

"That was children," she answered shortly. "Adult chicken pox can become pneumonia. In some cases fatal. Bring him in today."

Fatal! The melodramatic in me came out in full force. Before I even got back to the bedroom I had imagined the hearse, the funeral and the agony of life beyond. Sometimes I forget how much I love Steven, but it only takes a couple of minutes imagining life without him to turn me around. Tears washed over my face and I tried to pull myself together before I entered the room. "I've made an appointment with the doctor in half an hour. Do you feel up to having a shower?"

"No!" he wailed. "And I can't go without my hair being washed! Can't the doctor come here?" It took a minute or two to calm him down.

"Listen, I'll bring a comb and some water and we'll sort it out. You can wipe down with a face cloth before you put your clothes on."

By the time I got him dressed, down the stairs and into the car he had nothing left, just sat in the passenger seat, slumped, with his eyes closed. I put his seatbelt on him and drove with shaking hands. What if I lost him?

The receptionist took one look at Steven, spots and pallor and all and took him into a private waiting room. She turned a glare of accusation on me before she left the room. I could hear her muttering but could not make out the words.

In the doctor's office Steven began to cry. "I'm sorry. It's just you're being so kind."

The doctor looked at me. "Is he normally very emotional?"

I shook my head.

"I think we'd better keep a close eye. I'll give you something for the temperature. Call me if it gets above 38.5. Ice blocks, anything to cool him down. Watch for delirium. And it's important someone is with him all the time."

I put a mental line through my calendar. Lucky I was feeling so fondly towards him.

"Thank you, Doctor. I think I can get better now."

She looked at me. I shrugged. "Call me if you have any concerns."

Wrapped up on the sofa, remote control in his hand, orange juice with a straw within reach, he looked just like one of the kids. I kissed him on the forehead. "Anything I can get you?"

He looked up at me with pleading eyes. "Can I have some banana cake?"

"Sure, Honey, anything you want."

30

A day or two later, Steven sleeping soundly, I took the chance to call Leman's Literary Agency.

"Ah, Tasha, I was meaning to call you. Release date for the book has been set for next Friday – there were some things the lawyers were arguing over but they've been resolved now. There's a television advertising campaign and stands for the bookshops, everything we can do without a tour – that will follow your interview, which will air on national radio the week after. Congratulations!"

National radio. My heart gave a little dance.

"Thank you, Kent, thank you so much!"

"I also have another job for you, slightly different. Perhaps it's best if you come in again."

"How about Thursday? Four o'clock?" Steven was getting better. Charlotte could ring me if there was any emergency.

"Yes, fine. I'll see you then."

"And Kent . . . did you have a chance to look at that draft I brought you."

"Of course, yes. I put it to one side. Wait a minute, I'll find it and we can talk."

My heart was beating fast - silly, since he'd already said he wouldn't take it himself.

"I've had a look through - it really works well, this process, doesn't it? A good, conversational feel, excellent structure, and easy enough to polish the language and grammar." He seemed to be talking more to himself than me. "I'm impressed."

"Thanks."

"As I said, not for us, particularly. There are a couple of agencies in Auckland you could try, I'll give you the details, or would you like me to send it on myself?"

"Oh, Kent, yes please!"

"Failing that, I'd self-publish if I were you. Not something I should recommend, really, a disloyalty to the industry, but I've looked up your chap on the Internet, and he's really quite an authority. The margins for the author on self-published works are much higher, and there are many companies now who can arrange printing for you in short runs at low unit cost. If you like I can put you onto a very good editor, she's very quick, and then you just need someone to do the layout. So many of these self published books have far too little white space on the page . . ." Once again he seemed to forget there was anyone on the end of the line. I waited for him to complete his thought process. "I wonder . . . Yes, perhaps. Perhaps, my dear, should you choose to go down this route, we at Leman's can help you with layout. It's not usually the role of the literary agent but I do have some small experience. Yes. And we might tie that in with the other project I mentioned. Symbiosis. Yes."

He seemed to have run down.

"But we'll try the other agents first?"

"Yes, my dear, we'll try the other agents first. I will send it off tomorrow. If you could just get another copy to me, and a short biography of the author, and perhaps a synopsis, if that's not too much trouble."

"Synopsis?"

"A brief outline. So they can get an overview without reading the whole. Most useful."

I reached for a pad and pen. "Another copy, bio, outline. Thank you so much. I'll try to get these to you tomorrow." Would I get time to do them? I had never done a synopsis before. Another step on the learning curve.

"Anything wrong, my dear? You sound a little tired."

"Illness in the family, nothing serious, and we're coming out of it now. I'm so grateful."

"Not at all, not at all, a pleasure. I look forward to Thursday."

I went back to Steven and put a cold cloth on his forehead. He was still sleeping; he seemed calmer. The orange juice was empty so he must have woken at some point, but he hadn't called for me. I thought that was the first time since the day we saw the doctor.

"Oh, Steven," I whispered. "What would I do without you?" He squirmed slightly and settled again. I sat down on the floor and pressed the remote control. The movie he was watching started up. I turned the volume down. Benji. Movies from his childhood. He must really be feeling low.

31

With everything back to normal I marvelled at how productive I could be. I had four interviews lined up for this week and four for next. Kent's project was a book, one interview a week for twelve weeks, paid at full rate and a 10% split of the author's percentage.

"It's too generous."

"No it's not, my dear. Learn to accept it. You need to make money so you can stay in business. What good are you to us if you don't do that?"

The client was an international rock star and Bernard was spitting with jealousy. "Can't you get me an introduction, Tasha?"

"Maybe, let me talk to him first."

"But why me, Kent? There must be hundreds of ghost writers in England."

"Of course. But none with your very fine positive edge. We don't want a biography in the traditional sense, your format allows him to speak in his own voice about the parts of his life he wants to focus on."

"I don't know anything about him."

"And that's a plus, too, no preconceptions. He is very bored with being asked the same questions over and over again by people who want to paint him a certain way. This is a fresh start. Are you ready to do it?"

"Yes." A wide smile appeared on my face, and a spontaneous laugh escaped me. I could feel my cheeks pressing up below my eyes. "When can we start?"

This was my first time recording over the phone. Kent had got me an ultra-high quality phone system to give the best audio results. "As long as you can make out the words you'll be fine. At the present moment we don't plan to use the audio, and if we do in the end, well, people understand the concept of phone interviews, after all."

A rock star. Kent gave me some CDs and when I listened to them I was surprised how many tracks I recognised. These songs were made for soundtracks, lyrical stories in perfectly encapsulated form. I wrote that down so I would remember to compliment him.

Bernard and Kate were coming for dinner. The boys would barbeque, and I had bought a few pre-made vegetable dishes from the delicatessen. I found the easier I made things for myself, the less Bernard annoyed me. At six he and Steven rolled in the door laughing. "Kate not with you?"

"She bailed half way through the gig today."

"Why? I thought she usually hung around."

"Yeah, she does," said Steven. He turned away to take off his jacket.

"Guess she doesn't like competition." Bernard rocked his head back and forth with laughter.

I hate to encourage Bernard by reacting to him, he often throws out these fish-hook lines. I opened a pack of bread rolls and stacked them on a plate.

"Want to fire up the barbeque? I'm starving."

"Sure. Bern, text Kate, tell her we'll eat in 30 minutes."

Bernard opened the fridge and pulled out two beers. I hate it when he acts like he lives here – I ignored it as much as possible but my blood was rising. He took the tops off and wandered out onto the patio, texting without looking at the phone, like a teenager. I followed him to put plates and cutlery on the outdoor table.

"Dinner soon," I said as I passed in front of the television where Greta and Erica were glued to the screen. 'Watch the rest of that one then turn it off. And tell Charlotte."

Outside Bernard's phone beeped. "Uh. She says she's not coming."

"Why not?"

"Guess she's pissed at me."

"You don't seem very upset." He was still grinning, and my voice was tense with disapproval.

"After spending the afternoon in a strip joint, it's going to take quite a bit to kill the buzz."

My mouth fell open. Steven looked towards me, frozen, with his hand on the barbeque dial. Even the birds stopped singing.

"What?"

Steven's mouth opened and closed. Bernard let out another chuckle. I silenced him with a look that would have startled Medusa.

"What?" My voice was almost inaudible.

"I told you . . ."

"You told me?" My voice rose a little.

"Yes."

"Bernard, go inside." He obeyed. The glass door slid closed behind him.

"It's just stage time. Nowhere else is open in the afternoon, at least, not doing enough business for a band. I told you Kate was getting us whatever she could, for experience."

"Experience."

"Playing to an audience."

"So that's why you couldn't take the girls, why I've been on duty every afternoon for the past two weeks. You've been doing this for two weeks, ever since you went back."

Steven hung his head. "I told you."

I shook my head. I couldn't make out what he was saying. My anger had faded and in its place came a lifetime's rush of insecurity. First Kate – I knew she was more beautiful than me, despite how similar people said we were. I had almost got used to feeling mousy and invisible when she was around. But I couldn't stand the idea of Steven in a room full of young, attractive women all with the intention of pleasing the male eye.

"Look, there's historic precedent. The Beatles got their experience in the Red Light district of Hamburg."

I glanced up at him, just long enough for him to realise he wasn't helping. "I'm going to bed."

I crawled up the stairs and got straight under the covers without taking off my clothes. My sobs clawed their way out of somewhere very deep, but made hardly any noise. As far as I could consciously think of anything, I hoped Steven would follow me, but instead I heard the clattering of the barbeque, the children being called to dinner, the hum of conversation. Bernard's occasional barking laugh made me curl tighter every time. I hated him. I just wanted him to leave.

Sooner than normal I heard the door slam with his customary jarring bang. I breathed a little freer. Next I heard Steven's footsteps on the wooden stairs. He sat down on the bed next to me. "Babe . . ."

I turned towards him and pressed my face to his leg.

"Come here." He pulled me up and pressed me close to his body, arms inside his hug. "Tasha, I don't even see them."

I shook my head. I doubted it was true, but this was about more than just these girls. It was about me. I am such an innocent, no idea how to be attractive, sexy, flirt even. It's a wonder I ever got a husband at all! I'm so dowdy and boring and sad. Whenever I even try a sexy walk, or to catch a guy's eye and bat my eyelashes I feel like such a fool. I had watched Kate for years, she made it look so effortless. I would never be able to do it.

"I'm sorry! I'm sorry I'm not sexy and beautiful! I don't know why you don't leave!"

I felt his diaphragm twitch, but if he had the urge to laugh, he held it very well. He brushed my hair back from my face. "Tasha, I love you. I'm here."

Yeah, maybe. "Are you going to keep working there?"

"We have two more weeks booked. I'd like to keep going. Three hours on stage a day is really improving us. If it's okay with you."

I took a deep breath. "Okay." I said, and he gave me another squeeze.

"Here, come down for dinner. I'll set the girls up doing something in their room." He took my hand and pulled me up from the bed. I clung onto him for a few moments.

"Thank you."

He kissed me on the forehead and lead me downstairs.

32

"I want to learn to flirt and be sexy. How do I learn that?"

Wendy didn't bat an eye, just took a moment to consider the question. "Modelling."

"I can't be a model."

"No, I mean, model yourself on someone who is how you want to be."

"What do you mean?"

"Well, who would you define as being sexy – a woman, I mean, say a movie star?"

Hmm. "Catherine Zeta Jones. Selma Hayek. Angelina Jolie."

"Okay, so pick one of those and copy what they do. Get out some movies and watch how they move, their facial expressions. That will give you everything you need."

She really is a genius.

I would have to watch the movies while the children were at school. I got out Lara Croft, Mr and Mrs Smith, Playing by Heart and watched one each day. I watched the way Angelina Jolie walked, different when she was being watched than when she wasn't, the way she smiled for herself when no-one was looking and for effect when they were. I watched the way she moved, every muscle under control. Hmm. I would have to do something, some exercise, to really get this right.

I hate running but I found some music with a good beat on my iPod, dug out my old trainers and bought a streamlined Nike jacket with a headphone slot in the pocket. As soon as I dropped the girls off each morning I went out, compromising by running for the first minute of each track and walking the rest. That was okay. I could do that. Half an hour.

I thought about Angelina Jolie as I ran and felt my shoulders automatically pull back, my chest push out, my stomach pull in and my legs move with more purpose to each step, more in control. I can actually do this.

It was much harder with other people around. I started just walking with a little more sway to my hips when Steven was in the room, and holding my stomach tight.

One day he found my stash of videos. "What have you been watching? These are boy movies," he blurted, then clenched his teeth and stared at me warily.

I was in a different space now, not so vulnerable, especially since the strip bar work was finished. "They're training videos. I've been watching them." I took them out of his hand and put them back in the drawer. "None of your business." And I flashed him a little Angelina smile.

I was feeling pretty pleased with myself that day anyway – we had recorded my first television interview, with Winnie, and it had gone brilliantly well.

The effect of the book had been like a splash in slow motion. Kent had explained the strategy to me.

"Mystique. Just like with you, we wanted people to assume W.D. Hero was an adult man, and have the real fact be a surprise, something that people first whisper - could it be true? - then once they are sure, exclaim over. I want them saying 'You've got to read it, you won't believe it was a teenage girl.' So we're starting slow, but not too slow; displays in the book stores, your radio interview, book signings. Get people talking."

It was working just like he said, the public's slumbering curiosity was waking, brushing the sleep out of its eyes. When the time was just right, when the story was small enough and new enough but beginning to brew, Kent approached the television station of his choice and told them there was competition. He offered them the interview. But Winnie would only have me.

"She does know I've never done television before?"

"She knows what she is doing. She likes your sympathy and she trusts you."

"Well then, okay."

Winnie was paying me herself, $5,000. I was totally over the moon.

The T.V. station made a big deal of the interview, leading up to it with a week of advertising. A young, brilliant, female, probably criminal mind reforming was something totally new, and her looks, articulation, poise made excellent television. The mothers at the school gate started looking at me with interest, and one or two of the braver ones came over to ask if the interviewer they had seen on the advertisements was me.

I've never got into the mother culture, making myself unnecessarily lonely by standing off from the gossip. I put it down to being traumatised by vicarious competition when Charlotte was a toddler. Then she went through a phase of biting other children. Great attention-grabber, demonstrating superior intelligence if you look at it from that perspective, but the biter's mother is always an outcast. The tigress comes out in the victim's parent and it's only centuries of civilisation that stops them from pulling the perpetrator's arms off. So we stopped going to the toddler group and I was left to learn my parenting alone. The habit stayed with me even when the biting stopped, which it soon did. Charlotte's really a very refined and charming child.

But now, I was interesting, a bit of a trophy, and I found myself with invitations to coffee or the gym. I declined as politely as possible, loving the sound of the words that came out of my mouth. "My interviewing career is really taking off now, until I can take on an assistant my time is very full." Smiling nods of approval. Weak of me to enjoy them so much.

The interview aired on the Thursday night. I watched it with all my family around me, too happy to even resent the presence of Bernard. He and Kate had made up. "I knew what he was when I picked him, and he's improving, really."

I shrugged. I had yet to notice.

"It just got too much, watching his eyes roam from breast to breast without a pause in between to glance at me. It was all part of the plan, that once they got more comfortable on stage they could focus on audience rapport. Just I hadn't calculated on the topless waitresses."

I gripped the kitchen bench I was leaning on. Topless waitresses – one more little fact for me to absorb.

"Plus you know the way women are with musicians, it wasn't all him."

My fingers squeezed tighter. I could feel the texture of the surface indenting my skin.

"Anyway, I was stupidly jealous. It took me a day or two to recover."

I tried to relax my grip, to push myself away from the bench before I became permanently attached. "I don't know how you could stand there and watch it, even for a minute. It's driving me crazy enough and I wasn't even there."

Kate looked surprised. "Honey . . ." She put out a reassuring hand, which I evaded, blowing out a breath.

"At least they're finished there now."

"Yes."

I let the equivocation in her agreement slide for now. I wanted to get back to the happy mood of today's success.

"Mum, it's starting," Charlotte called, and Kate and I found seats in the living room, Kate on the arm of Bernard's chair. I watched as she draped her body against his shoulder. I still hadn't mastered that one. I sat awkwardly on the sofa next to Steven. He took my hand. Greta climbed onto his knee.

It was weird watching myself. I noticed I turned my watch around and around on my wrist at the start, when I was nervous, but as the interview progressed I got engrossed in what Winnie was saying and relaxed. Really I looked quite intelligent as I nodded and smiled. Hard to believe they had filmed the nods and smiles afterwards. In the wide shots I thought I looked bigger than I really am. It got worse as the interview progressed and I relaxed on screen. 20 minutes in it was too much to bear. "I'm fat!" I wailed. "Look at my stomach."

The response was varied. "No you're not, Mum." My sweet matter of fact Charlotte; "The camera always adds five kilograms," Kate; "Be quiet, I want to listen." Bernard. Steven just squeezed my hand and continued to stare at the screen. I turned to look at him for a moment, then kept my eyes on him. I liked the expression on his face. Respect. He turned to me and smiled. "You're great!"

The program finished and a big cheer went up.

"Wow, Mum, you're on T.V." said Greta, hugging me. "All my friends will be so jealous."

"Celebration called for." Steven stood up and headed for the kitchen with Kate following.

"I've come prepared." She pulled a wrapped bottle from the fridge and took the paper off. Champagne. Veuve Cliquot.

She handed the bottle to Bernard to open and found some glasses. There was something in that for me to notice, of course she could have opened it herself, but the gesture was feminine, and I watched Bernard's pride swell a notch as he took it from her.

"To my little sister!"

"By five minutes!"

"Even so. To her brilliant success! And I'm taking credit for part of it. In fact most of it."

"You're so full of rubbish."

The champagne went straight to my happy head. I swayed to the sofa and sank onto it, calling for potato chips. My darling husband put down his glass and went out to the supermarket to get me some. I think maybe it's the first time I've ever really felt loved.

33

It was my fourth interview with Blue King, the English rock star. He was charming, flirty, and we always chatted for a few minutes before we started recording. I was trying my Angelina persona with him, it was much easier on the phone, and especially because we had never met and he had never known me as anything else. It added an edge when we started the interview, too, brought out an element of mischief, an apparently careless honesty. The Flirt approves of everything.

We had spent a couple of sessions before we started the interviews proper talking about what he wanted to say in the book, the parts of himself and his life that he wanted people to understand.

"I want them to get that everyone can live their dreams, it just takes work and focus and sticking with it. But that sounds trite and clichéd, so I can't just say it, I have to show them."

"So how do you want to do that? Any ideas?"

"I think we just start out with my life before. I didn't have any big breaks. So talk about what life was like, about realising I really loved music, the years of practice, the knocks, and picking myself up and keeping going." He hesitated. "Then about Barry dying, I want to give the true story about that." There was an edge to his voice that I hadn't heard before. I opened my mouth to speak but then let the moment pass. "And then go on to the start of success, the first breaks, meeting my manager – that was at one of my long slogs at a grotty bar in Glasgow – and how things took off from there. I couldn't have been anything else than what I am. If I thought about giving up, taking an easy job, having a normal life, I just felt so sick I couldn't do it. I want to say all that. I really want people to understand."

"Blue . . ."

"What is it, sweetheart?"

"Look, you know Kent asked me to not research about you before doing this, so I wouldn't be coloured by what has already been written."

"Yeah, it's great."

"So . . . what was that about Barry dying? You sounded . . . like you'd been betrayed."

There was a long pause. "Well, that was the scandal, wasn't it?" Another pause. I held my breath, suppressing an indecent curiosity, telling myself I had a professional need to know this. "We'll have to address it in the book, even though I'm sick of talking about it." I was glad he couldn't see my face. Does avidity communicate down a phone line? "Well . . . I was accused of murdering him. My best mate."

I exhaled as quietly as possible. He sounded so sad. "Poor you."

"Yeah . . . I was acquitted at trial, but a lot of people still believe it."

I felt so sorry for him, and then, horribly, suspicion crept in. How did I know what was true? I thought about Winnie, about Kent, and wondered exactly where his limits were for the whitewash service. "That must be awful."

"Yeah . . . anyway, that's a big part of what I want to set straight. Or get past."

For a day or so after this conversation I had examined my morals once again, my responsibilities. Would I just facilitate whatever someone wanted to say? It was all about spin, after all, about making someone credible, presenting them in the best light. What if he were lying? What sort of position could that put me in? Well, what if he were telling the truth, and I were just the next person to betray him?

In the end I decided it couldn't be any worse than Winnie. This was only one murder, after all, and possibly not even that. Then I caught the thought, ashamed to own it. I had no evidence that Winnie had done anything wrong.

Blue was a little down. "Yeah, my Mum's not well."

"You're close?"

"Well, you know, I've been busy the last couple of decades." He gave the short laugh I had come to recognise as his guilt signal.

"You're too hard on yourself."

"You don't understand about my Mum."

"Well then, tell me. Shall I hit record."

This wasn't on the plan for today, but my gut said to go for it.

"Okay."

"Blue King talks to Tasha Stuart in a series of one-on-one conversations. You can read more about Blue at www.blue-king.co.uk. Tasha Stuart is a professional interviewer, www.tashastuart.co.nz.

"Blue, you said you'd been thinking about your mother. She contributed to your career?"

"Yeah, she's not well at the moment, so she's on my mind. I'm hoping to get up to see her early next week, but in the meantime I've been thinking back over the years. I've said there wasn't much money at home, and we lived outside a remote village, Dad was a part-time gamekeeper on a big estate. The owners only came up two weeks a year for the shooting, all that house for two weeks a year, and we lived in a cottage owned by them. It was stone, tiny windows, central heating worked as long as it wasn't too cold outside, and there was food as long as Dad could catch it. Mum was terrified he'd be caught poaching and lose his job.

"Anyway, there we were, and I wanted music lessons. Well, who teaches electric guitar in a remote Yorkshire village? There was a piano teacher, though, a real dragon, and an old piano in the church hall. Mum cleaned for the piano teacher to pay for the lessons, and came down to the hall with me each day so I could practice. It was a half hour walk and once we got there it was freezing. She sat knitting pieces to sell in the post office shop. Once a year she'd do me a pair of fingerless gloves to keep me warm while I played. And she always said how much she loved hearing me, even when I was awful and she would have been far warmer at home.

"Then, when I was eleven, I finished at the village school and took the bus to the nearest town, to the comprehensive. As soon as I was there I asked around for a guitar teacher. I found one, but then it was extra for the lessons and extra for the late bus, and I was so desperate to have a guitar of my own.

"Mum took more cleaning jobs to pay for it all. Dad didn't like it, but he doesn't say much, my Dad. So she kept going, and I was grateful, but I guess I took it for granted, just let her work that extra hard for me. I couldn't do anything else."

"She sounds wonderful."

"She is."

"And what then?"

"When I was fifteen I joined a band. I needed to be in town for rehearsals, and just in case we got a gig. I told my Mum I was leaving home. Well, my Dad wouldn't have it, he forbad it. So I just packed my bags and went, left school, got a part time job, slept wherever I could find room. I didn't go back for two years. I sent Mum a postcard with my address once I had one, six months later, and she came to visit, came to listen to the band, and never once told me I'd broken her heart. I asked her about that, once. You know what she said?"

"Tell me."

"She said 'It would have broken my heart if you'd stayed. I know you did what you needed to do to be happy.'"

"And I said 'So you don't miss me then, Mum?' and I smiled a cheeky smile. And that's the first time I ever saw her cry."

There was silence at the end of the phone. My heart was like a stone in my chest. I thought of my own children. Could I let them follow their dreams like she did?

"And what about now?"

"Well, Dad's not been great for a few years now, his short term memory's not good, so when I wanted to buy them a house, move them nearer to me, and into some luxury, she wouldn't do it, said Dad needed to stay in a place he knew. I bought the house they live in, modernised it, so it's warm now, and light, and added a conservatory. But Mum's still looking after Dad, she won't go out because he gets confused when she's not there. I think she's just very, very tired."

"I bet she still loves it when you come home."

He laughed. "It's like a time warp. Going back to my bedroom as it was when I was fifteen, single bed in the attic. I put in a skylight so I can see out to the world, but I still have to climb a ladder to go to sleep at night. And me, a big star!"

He roared with laughter now. I reached out to turn off the recorder, but something stopped me, and then he was speaking again, very quiet now.

"It was Mum who was hardest hit when I was taken to prison. It was only a night or two until I got out on bail but she said she was in torment, imagining her little boy there, and afraid. And I was afraid, very afraid of spending a chunk of my life in there, but I really believe she went through worse. She came to visit in Glasgow while I was waiting for the trial. It was a horrible time. And all I felt from her was love. All I've ever felt from her was love. 'I didn't do it, Mum, you know I didn't. He was my mate, my best mate. It was an accident, and I don't know how to get through.' "

The anguish in his voice was heart-wrenching, I felt like I was there in the room with his mother as he spoke.

"And she put her arms around me and held me like I was a little boy again."

34

So we had broached the topic of the scandal. With my spin doctor's hat on I thought we couldn't have started it from a more sympathetic angle. This loving son wouldn't lie to his mother. So he must be telling the truth. I talked to Kent about the progress.

"Excellent! Yes! I couldn't have thought of a better approach. Well done, Tasha!"

I was going to disclaim credit but was learning to take compliments when they were offered. His honesty possibly had something to do with me, after all.

"I have another assignment for you, too, Tasha, simpler this time. Another radio interview for a completed book. Shall I send it over for you to read?"

"Yes, great, what is it?"

"You'll see. And at the same time, would you record the author reading excerpts? Not your usual brief, I know, but should be simple enough."

"Sure, easy."

"I'll mark the relevant passages in the copy I send."

"And it's to be used where?"

"There is a website. We're trying a new approach to the first splash, viral email marketing in conjunction with some fairly big names in the subject area. It's not live yet, but I'll let you know." There was a pause before he continued. "Everything well at home?" Was there an edge to his question?

"Yes, fine."

Except it wasn't. I felt I was losing touch, getting busier and my grip on the children and the household was slipping.

Steven picked up the girls every afternoon now, while I was working either in my office at home with my headphones on or in the little soundproof room Kent had rented for me while the Blue King interviews continued. I was ashamed to admit how much I loved being there, airtight, silent, no possibility of interruption. In my head I knew I loved my family but sometimes going back into the chaotic, multi-conversation environment made me recoil, gave me the urge to run.

Kate was having fun spending time with the girls, and they loved being with her watching the boys play. Yesterday I came home to find all three of them in matching spangled backless tops, Kate conducting while the girls performed a song and dance routine, Bernard on the piano shouting encouragement.

"What . . ?"

"Mum, Mum, come and watch!"

Their faces were shining, so happy, I couldn't be the dragon and tell them to stop and get changed. I'd seen Kate wearing an identical top, I'd thought it slutty, even on her.

They pulled me to the sofa and sat me down.

"Bernard, on three," Erica ordered, and snapped her fingers twice. The song started again. I sat primly on the front of my seat, but I couldn't maintain my disapproval. They were great. I can't hold a tune, but I can hear when music is good, and they were fantastic: note-perfect with harmonies, and the song was one I loved, from Lilac's newest album. The dance moves were simple and very effective. They took up the whole of the tiny space with confidence and beautiful, beautiful joy.

They crowded around me when they had finished, hugging me tight. I applauded loudly, Kate and Bernard joining in.

"Fantastic – you guys are so talented." They giggled. Greta started running in circles, wound up with adrenaline. I could see the beginnings of overload. She's only six. "Time to get changed for bed now." I wanted them out of those costumes and back fully clothed again. "Where's Daddy?"

"Getting takeaways," Kate answered. "Rehearsal went late. We have some big news."

"Let me tell her!"

"No, me!"

"No, me!"

"Okay, first one changed can tell me. Pyjamas on, I'll wait here."

They tumbled over themselves to get out of the room. Kate opened her mouth, hesitated. "I guess I better let them tell you, but I'm bursting."

I looked over at Bernard. He was beaming too."

"I'm glad there's good news. But Kate, those tops, what were you thinking?"

"What's the big deal?" she asked, in genuine surprise. "You let them run around on the lawn naked."

"That's different!" I hissed, "And anyway, Charlotte doesn't do that any more."

"They liked the top when I wore it, said I looked like a movie star. It only took an hour to run up another three for them. They were ecstatic."

"They're children! They look like tarts!"

"Like I do?"

"Let's not go there."

The look of fury on her face did not intimidate me as it would once have. I was about to say more when I heard running footsteps in the hall.

"Café Storm is going to play in front of Lilac!"

There were wails from the two who hadn't got it out first, and a shove or two before I could break it up.

"What do you mean?"

I turned as Bernard spoke "Support band. For the Lilac tour in May – three concerts: Auckland, Wellington, Christchurch. The New Zealand tour manager came to rehearsal today."

I looked at Kate for confirmation. She nodded, her grin returning.

"Oh. My. God!"

Steven arrived home with fish and chips and another bottle of champagne. "I had to go to three shops to find a cold one."

I threw my arms around him. "This is wonderful news."

He pulled back and looked me in the face. "Yeah. And best for me, it's money again. I know it's been tough on you, the pressure to pay the bills pretty much on your own."

"But we've been fine, huh?" I noticed in passing how easy it was to look him in the eye now. When had that changed?

"So how did it happen?"

"Kate, you tell her, it was all you." I turned to her, my mouth open.

"Well, you know we recorded a couple of songs last month. We're getting near ready to put out an album, we just need the money to do it. I started sending the demo disc out to everyone I could think of, and then a few weeks ago I heard they were looking for local tour support for Lilac. So I made some calls, talked to the guy in Auckland, played a bit over the phone and he asked me to send it up. He liked it, sent it to Lilac for approval, and she sent him down to listen. He came into the café today, stayed three hours. A really nice guy."

"If you like them in that James Bond kind of style. Doesn't look like a rock tour manager." Bernard's voice was grumpy, his eyebrows low. Kate got up and sat on his knee. The angry mask fell away and I saw a look of adoration breeze across his face. Then she jumped up again.

"But you're right, he was cute." She tweaked Bernard's cheek and turned, not seeing the moment of heart-breaking sadness before the scowl returned. At that moment I almost liked him.

"Coffee, Bernard?"

"Yeah, thanks Tasha."

"Kate, Steven?"

Kate shook her head and sprawled across the sofa.

"I'll make it," Steven said, getting up. "Will you have one?"

"Yeah, I'll come, too."

I watched as Steven started to heat the milk. "Wow, Lilac!"

"Yeah!" He turned to me, his eyes shining. "This could be it."

35

"Talking of money, Hon, how are we doing?"

"Pretty good. You brought in $600 last month, and Kent paid me last week for the Blue King interviews, so that was $2700 in a lump. I think we have a couple of thousand dollars in the bank after the bills come out this month, maybe three, even though we've been fairly free with the champagne the last week or two."

Steven didn't reply, just stared down at the floor.

"What do you need?"

"I think it's time to record an album. Kate thinks we're ready, and I do, too. But she thinks we should wait for a recording contract and I disagree. That could be a while coming and I know we could be selling albums at the gigs we do. People have been asking for months. It's okay for her, she's got no responsibilities. We have five people to take care of."

"So how much do you think you need?"

"Depends. We need someone talented to produce the tracks. Paying them full rate is out of the question, but Bernard's got a mate who's pretty good, and he likes Kate, she could talk him into a reduced rate, I'm sure. That's a delicate balance for Bernard, he's got to keep civil with the guy and he's already jealous as hell with Kate – she really knows her moves doesn't she?"

This sent my mind on a different, familiar track, but Steven brought me back, continuing. "Anyway we'd need a recording studio for at least a week. Maybe we can cut the cost by recording late, in the down time. I don't know, maybe $30,000."

I leaned against the bench, my head spinning. "What about Bernard?"

"The band has been a year with next to no income. He spent what he had months ago. He's been borrowing just to live."

"And Scott?"

"I think he's got it but he's too cagey with it to spend on this. I think it's just us, Babe. Can we do it? Maybe borrow on the house?"

My stomach sank but at the same time there was a curious seductive appeal about the idea. I loved the thought that Steven would take a risk with the family for what he loved. I had done it, and felt bad every second. For a moment I gloried in the idea of being understanding and sympathetic when it went wrong. Then I considered the alternative, that it would work out brilliantly. I couldn't lose.

I smiled. "Sure."

Steven's eyes widened with disbelief, then he swung me around, my feet bumping the cupboards.

"There goes the bigger house for another year or two, if we can even get a bigger mortgage. Goodness knows who'd give us one."

No-one, as it turned out. I came back from my appointment with the third mortgage broker and told Steven the news.

He looked down at the table. "Oh well, that's that, I guess. We'll just have to wait a while longer."

"Don't give up. I'll keep trying."

He gave me a wan smile. "Thanks." A minute later he picked up the magazine he was reading and went to lie on the sofa.

I wasn't feeling the best myself. Apart from the blow from the mortgage broker there had been an incident at school that day. It was the first time I had picked the girls up in a couple of weeks. I had gone into Greta's classroom looking for her, since she wasn't at the gate with the others. Another mother was there, with her daughter who was crying. Greta stood defiant. The teacher turned to me. "Ah, Mrs Wendel."

"My name's Stuart, Tasha Stuart. Call me Tasha."

"I'm sorry," she pretended, "I should have remembered. I wanted to talk to you. We had a little occurrence today, with Greta. She hasn't been kind to Victoria, and we've been asking her to apologise."

I turned to Greta and crouched down. The teacher and the other mother looked very big from down here. "What happened, Honey?"

Victoria's mother sniffed. I kept my eyes on Greta's face.

Greta looked at me and her expression softened. "I don't want to play with her, and I won't say sorry. She's a wimp, cries at nothing. And then she's mean, for no reason. I don't have to be her friend."

"Now, Greta," interjected the teacher, "we're all friends here. We include everybody. It's kind to let others join in your games."

"But I don't want to. Auntie Kate says if I don't want someone in my games I don't have to."

"I'm sure your Auntie Kate wouldn't want you to be unkind. Ms . . . Tasha, perhaps you would ask Greta to apologise. Otherwise we shall have to consider punishment. And perhaps you would have a talk to her Auntie Kate about the behaviour expected at school."

I took a deep breath. For a second I thought about doing what she asked. Greta stared at me, pleading and strong at the same time. "No, Mrs Walsh. Greta doesn't want to apologise. Victoria isn't hurt. There will be no punishment. In this case I agree with my sister. As far as I'm concerned, Greta is perfectly free to choose her own friends. We'll see you tomorrow."

Greta squeezed my hand as I took hers and we turned and walked away.

I felt a complex mix of emotions: triumph, and unease. Something was shifting, in me and in Greta. This had the flavour of "Charlotte the Biter", but this time I had stood up for my daughter instead of fearfully hiding from the world. I was out of my comfort zone, in unchartered territory . . .

36

$30,000. Where was I going to get it? Who did I know who had that kind of money? What about Kent? I was sure he would have, but was it crossing a professional line to bring this up with him? Come to think of it, Winnie and Blue would also easily have it. No, that was definitely out. Maybe I'd just talk to Kent about it, hypothetically, ask his advice about where to go.

The more I thought about it the more excited I was at the prospect of enabling the recording to happen. I sometimes felt a little left out of the whole band thing, and it would make me feel really good to bring in some real money, even if it was just a loan.

Business was ticking along well, a fairly steady stream of short interviews and I had another book project which meant repeat appointments over several weeks. I had joined a lunchtime network group and a few referrals were starting to come from there. I still did my five calls each day, with some success, though nothing like what Kate had produced; there had been some repeat business over the last month or two, and some calls from people clients had spoken to. I often hit the $2000 mark in a given week, and loved it when that happened.

So what was I looking for? Was this enough for me? Where did I want the business to go? Actually, at the moment it felt pretty good just as it was. The interviews were fascinating and I loved meeting the wide range of people: business owners to consultants to psychologists to, well, rock stars and criminals, oops, I mean, business women. There was enough variety just in that to keep me satisfied for a long time.

What about ambition, though? I tried to keep it buried and it continually poked green shoots through. If I told myself at night to keep it cool, to spend more time with the kids, to take it easy, to take a day off, then woke next morning from dreams of capture, imprisonment, and eventual escape. Those escape dreams were exhilarating, and I looked guiltily at my daughters as I gave them breakfast.

Okay, so ambition. Time to face the vision and see what it actually contained.

I took a pen and paper and wrote "What I want" at the top.

Everything I had written on the list with Wendy I had achieved. It looked small and cowardly now. "What do I want that is bigger than this?"

I closed my eyes. A bigger house. A red Porsche Boxster. To travel internationally to do an interview. To sell an interview transcript to an international magazine.

Something was wrong, it felt like clockwork. There was no Dopamine rush, no tiny edge of terror that told me this was it, this was what I had to do next. I looked at my list again and realised that at that moment I didn't actually care about anything. I didn't care if I ever moved or felt anything again.

I heard Steven downstairs. He started the vacuum cleaner; I clenched my teeth. I was working. I needed quiet. I knew he thought I had let the housework slip.

I felt goddess anger welling in me, resentment echoing back and forth between us as he tidied the house in passive aggressive silence and I just wanted him gone. He had the back door open and cold air blew under the bedroom door. I pulled my robe over my legs but the hateful breeze still attacked my face. I wanted to explode. This list was my life at this moment, this was where I defined who I was and it wasn't working. I wanted a target for my wrath. My nose twitched.

So let it out.

I hated being married. I hated being tied to one place by the responsibility of children and schooling. I hated having to sit in a room full of people and connect on demand. Be available. Be sympathetic. Compromise my life. Apologise for my life. Justify my life for these strangers.

If I were alone I would live in a bach someplace by the sea, wrapped in a blanket through the winter, watching the waves with my hands wrapped around a coffee mug, being entirely and completely me, every minute. I would talk to no-one, think of no-one, answer to no-one, just watch the waves and think my thoughts. I could get by on a packet of toast bread and a tin of spaghetti every couple or three days. I would finally lose the weight I didn't want without having to distract myself from this life I never asked for.

Is it too much to ask to be alone? I want to run away, to not be bothered, for no-one to have any expectations of me. I don't give a damn about the house and the car and the fancy clothes – even the international travel I can do without, if I can just be alone. God, even if I could just have silence. Just turn off the fucking vacuum cleaner and let me think. Close the damn outside door and get this air out of my face.

The noise stopped and I breathed for a moment, but then Steven's step creaked on the landing, he opened the door and stood there, vacuum in hand. A dangerous thing to do. I turned my glare towards him and gave my head a single shake. The door banged and the noise started again, much closer. I heard the chair scrape in my office and the sound of papers tumbling across the floor. There was a loud bang, a thud, the vacuum stopped again. Against my will my ears strained to hear what was happening. There was that one big pile of stuff I had promised Susan, the organiser, I would sort out after she had gone. Steven was trying to balance it back up again. I could hear his screaming silence: "For God's sake, Tasha, get this place sorted!"

"Get out of my space," I screamed silently in return. The office door banged and I heard Steven's footsteps going downstairs, the vacuum cord dragging and clattering behind him.

Finally, silence. Then the pipes in the wall behind me started whining. He was doing the dishes. Enough. Keeping my eyes from him as I passed through the kitchen, lest I kill him with their spark, I grabbed the car keys from the hook by the door. "I'm going out," I muttered. I didn't care if he heard me, I thought he could probably guess.

We live in Beckenham and in minutes I was up Cashmere Hill, away from the houses on Dyers Pass Road. I turned right onto the Summit Road and asked my little car for everything it had. The twists and winds were wildly satisfying, long visibility, and corners that camber well. Complete focus lets you drive this road fast, at the forward edge of control, with comparative safety. This urge could easily become self-destructive if I tried to suppress it, but I let it flow in glorious freedom. Let the anger flow.

It's only in the last little while I have learned to do this, I used to think anger was dangerous, to be denied and destroyed. But it can't be denied and destroyed, it can only be channelled, into art or into action or into words.

There never is a cause for anger. We think there is. We look for someone to blame. But it rises naturally, spontaneously, only looking for a channel to pass through. I know this, but I forget. I felt it rising and then Steven started the vacuum cleaner in response. I should have got out of there sooner, only I didn't see what it was.

I don't hate my family. I know this. Only, when anger flows through me they need to be out of my way. Someone could get hurt. I need to get myself out of the way. I turned up the music, a blast of Cold Play. Let this wild energy flow!

By the time I reached Gebbies Pass the ebb was underway. I turned right down into the valley and followed the winds to the valley floor where I took a gravel road to the left, twisting into the depths of nowhere. I stopped the car, turned off the engine, let the dust and the silence settle.

After a minute I could hear birds. I wound down the window an inch to let the sound expand. I closed my eyes. Now, in the nothing, there was space for me.

Ambition. Like Dr Jekyll's monster it was roaring, breaking free of its bonds. There wasn't any clear form to it yet, it was hazy, as though seen through fog. This was the first glimpse I'd had that it was so huge. I thought I was content. To earn money, to pay my way, a few nice clothes. But this was something different, something orders of magnitude different, something that had yet to take shape. More unchartered territory. How would I do this? I had no idea how to do this. Something in me said to just let it happen, but how? What would that be like? This was a part of me I did not recognise, or know how to take responsibility for, or how to nurture.

The time was past when I could have stuffed it back where it came from, kept it the tiny seed it had seemed until now. The monster was out, and for the moment I was too scared to look at it, to know it, to acknowledge it as my own.

And then I felt myself smile. I realised "I want this . . . I've always wanted this, only I've been too afraid."

I sat back in my seat and smiled again. I laughed. "Let it come then. Let it be." I felt my arms raising and got out of the car. Fists held high like a vertical Superman I turned on the spot, eyes closed, until my face was full in the midday sun. "Let it be!"

37

Pah! $30,000. I would earn it myself. On the way home I sold my car, bought a second-hand moped. I handed Steven the $7,000 as I walked in the door. He looked pretty silly, standing there in my floral apron, mouth hanging open, the wad of cash in his hand.

"Where?"

"I sold the Corolla. That'll be enough to get you started on the recordings, and I'll find a way to get the rest. It's time to get things moving. I needed a kick up the pants to get my business going faster. It was getting too easy."

Steven stared. I grinned back. I probably looked a bit manic.

"You sold the Corolla?"

"Yeah." My grin widened. "What's more important: a car or your future?"

Steven started to grin, too.

"But what will you drive? How will you get around?"

"I bought a moped. You know I've always wanted one. The girls can walk to school. We'll make it work."

It was slowly sinking in. "We can start? Wow!" And then he finally got it. I laughed, and he picked me up and swung me around. "You'd do that for me!" But it wasn't a question, it was a triumphant statement.

Charlotte came into the room. "What's happening?"

Steven waved the cash in her face. "Mum's got us the money to start the album!"

Charlotte looked uncertainly from Steven to me. "That's cool, Dad, but don't lose it, will you?"

She turned and walked back to the living room. We watched her go, such perfect sang-froid, and then we began to laugh.

What I want:

To pay for the album myself, $30,000+

To be paid to travel internationally for an interview

A red Porsche Boxster

A bigger house

A gorgeous body

Beautiful clothes

To be interviewed myself, on TV.

That would do for now. Amazing how differently I felt about the car and the house now that I knew myself. I spent the afternoon lying on the sofa imagining living in the dream house, walking from room to room to room, revelling in bathrooms the size of my current bedroom, gliding down wide sweeping staircases in a black sequinned dress. I looked through fashion magazines with a critical eye, not to despise, but to desire. I want to look like that, in that dress, with those eyes, shaded in smoky grey. I found an old Vogue with Angelina Jolie on the cover, wearing a striking red dress that you hardly noticed because of the magnetic draw of her face. How did she do that? How was she more present in a fading photographic image than I had ever felt in real life? Until now. Now I was starting to feel how it was done.

I imagined waiting in an airport lounge for my flight to be called, my minimal hand luggage and stylish new handbag at my side. I had my voice recorder in my handbag, but this would be a live interview, an international conference, a world renowned authority on the stage for me to bring live into the room. Perhaps someone who didn't usually speak; or someone who was tired of the standard lecture and wanted a less formal format; or . . . who cared? There were a hundred ways it could happen. I wriggled back into the sofa cushions, a cat-like smile on my face.

TASHA STUART INTERVIEWS . . .

38

It was time to crank up the marketing calls. I asked Kate to give me a hand. "The more I get, the sooner the album gets finished."

"Okay. But you know I still think we could have waited for a recording company contract."

"This is faster, you know it is."

"And faster is always better?"

"Since when did you develop patience?"

"Tasha, I feel like I don't know you any more."

"Liar! We're both like this, and you know it."

"Seriously, though, a few more months could give the guys a lot more polish. Especially with the extra motivation they've got with the Lilac tour. My gut tells me it would have been better to wait."

"But Steven thinks different."

"Steven thinks different. And Bernard is just happy going along, playing his music. Sometimes I wonder he ever got anywhere at all on his own."

"What about Scott?"

"Scott's very pleased, but he keeps it all pretty cool. After all this time he's still an enigma to me. Never asking Maria out but chuffed as hell when she asked him. Not pushing the recording or the gigs, or anything really, but there's a smouldering glow when anything good happens. Keeps it all under his hat. Was he like that when he worked for you?"

I thought back. "Yeah. He'd answer any question like he'd been thinking about it for days, but he almost never volunteered an opinion. He's clever, talented, but not a big go-getter."

"Well, I suspect he's pretty keen for Café Storm to be a big success. And he's got a clear idea of how that's going to look. Just a minimal wince if he doesn't like something, a wider grin when he feels we're on the right track, a tiny throw-away comment, like when he thought we'd done enough old people's homes and schools. He said "Fine up till now, but enough. We can do better." And he was right. Just said it once, just loud enough to hear, but there's an authority in those rare words that makes you stop and listen, and think."

"So everyone's okay with it except you?" I wondered if it was because it was me funding it, if she was jealous.

"Don't get me wrong, it's exciting, and Steven's right, we can sell them wherever we play. And I can take care of that, you know me, happy peddling a great product."

"Then what?"

"Like I said, it's just my gut. Something's not sitting exactly right."

Just like the first time, Kate's calls were ten times as successful as mine. The budget worked like this: we needed to bring in $1,500 a week to cover my overheads (small) and the household bills. Anything above that could go into the album. Steven's income was down slightly with recording, but still there would be a hundred or two most weeks.

In the first week of the scaled-up marketing we had huge success. The bookings for the next two weeks would give us nearly another $4,000 for the fund. I was ecstatic.

The plan was it would be paid back from the profits, 50% going to me and the rest split by the guys and Kate. None of us had any idea how long that would take, but selling them for $20 each, with $3 each in CD production costs, that meant $8.50 per copy coming back to me. Around 3,500 copies. How hard could that be? Especially with Kate on sales. I was optimistic. And apart from that I was profoundly, delightedly proud that I was funding it.

The other upside was Steven's mood. He had found his flow. He was loving the recording process and he came home with a bounce in his step every day.

39

I was nervous, wandering around the house unable to settle. I picked up a magazine and stared at the cover for over a minute before deciding to open it. A couple of minutes later it was back on the table, forgotten. I realised Charlotte had asked me something some time ago, and was vaguely aware that I had told her to wait.

"Sorry, what was that you asked?"

"I said, could I do some painting?"

"Of course, darling, you know where everything is."

"Can I move your papers off the table?"

Absently I picked them up myself. Maybe I would go and stare at the fax machine again for a while. That was where I felt most purposeful.

That afternoon I had had a meeting with the manager of a firm of insurance brokers, discussing a short video interview with each of their consultants. Al, the manager, would arrange the camera work "I'm a bit of a practised amateur" and I would sit off camera and put the subjects at ease, bring out their best.

"I liked what you did with Bruce, my business coach. He comes across really well in your interview, it really captures his enthusiasm, made me doubly sure I'm working with the right guy. Do you think you can do that with all my consultants?"

"It's my job to bring out their best side, their customer service commitment. It's what I love about my job."

"And the video is fine? I'd like to do each one in one take, if we can, it makes it much easier to process and a straight through sequence looks more honest – people wonder what was cut if they see an edit."

There were 20 in Christchurch, 20 in Wellington and 30 in Auckland. They were going to pay me $100 for each one plus travel expenses if he got the go-ahead from the directors. That meeting was this afternoon, and the contract would come by fax if it was approved.

I stood staring at the machine, chewing my lip for a minute or two. I really needed something else to do.

The laptop was slow to start, taking excruciating minutes to update the virus checker. I knew from experience there was no point starting any other applications while it was in progress, it would only end up confused and with 10 copies of everything trying to open at once, then the word processor format reverting to some prehistoric version with none of my painstakingly tailored styles.

My breathing was shallow and I could feel my heart thumping. Two voices in my head began to argue. I began to wonder if I were going mad.

"It's only $7,000, get a grip!"

"$7000 above normal. That pays for another 20% of the album. Plus travel paid."

"Yeah, I know. I know. But these nerves aren't helping anything."

What did Wendy say? When things are uncomfortable, take a step back and observe myself. Describe what is going on in words. "Oh, look, I'm nervous about the contract. My chest is tight, I'm breathing in my chest, not my belly. My sense of humour has been suspended. I think it's all very serious. I am focusing on the possibility of failure, not the possibility of success. Ah! I am also nervous about actually doing the interviews if I get them. I am thinking I might not be up to it. I am out of my comfort zone because the format is different. One take. No editing. But I'm not asking the question in a way that I can answer because I am in the middle of blind terror. Or I was."

I took a deep breath and blew it out. So I thought I wasn't sure if I could do it or not. Was that true? I laughed. No, I was sure I could do it. I would love it. Brilliant! I'm fine.

The phone chirped once and I nearly fell off my chair. A long pause – what if the fax machine didn't feed right, if this was the contract and it screwed up and then they wouldn't resend it? Then the rapid tapping of the paper feed and there it was, in my hand.

"Yay!"

"What Mum?" Charlotte called from downstairs.

"I got the contract!"

I ran downstairs waving it.

"What contract?"

"Interviews, 70 of them, $7000 for Daddy's album."

"Well done, Mum." Her coolness dulled me a little. Then I smiled.

"I'm going to celebrate. Cookies anyone?"

40

"Hello, Tasha, Kent here. How are you?"

"Fine. You?"

"Very well, very well." I sensed a little hurry in his voice, not his usual timeless calm. "Things going well with Blue, are they? How far would you say you are from finishing the preliminary interviews?"

"Four to go. We've been doing weekly calls whenever we can, but you know he's had a couple of concerts – we found his focus was on the event coming up, so we delayed two of the sessions. We'll be done in about a month - that was the plan, wasn't it?"

"It was indeed." There was an uncertain pause, again surprising as Kent is well prepared for every phone call.

"Kent?"

"My dear, I wonder if it's possible to speed things up a bit."

"Sure, from my perspective. It depends on Blue. What's up?"

"Nothing, precisely, I just have a feeling . . ."

"Well, why don't you suggest it to him? I'm flexible, we could do them in a couple of days if he has the time."

"Good, good." I could tell his mind was somewhere else, but then suddenly he was much more engaged. "But I'd prefer it if you would talk to

193

him about it. Do you think you could come up with a logical reason which would appeal to him, creatively? Yes, I think that's the best way to approach it."

The sides of my mouth stretched down as I considered. "Well, actually there is a good case for things coming together quickly at the end. It's happened naturally with a couple of other projects and it's very satisfying."

"Excellent. Well, see if you can persuade him, will you, and let me know? I'd be so grateful."

"Kent, what . . ?"

"I will tell you, if anything comes to anything. I'll expect to hear from you soon. Goodbye, Tasha, and thank you again."

I was about to hang up when Kent came back on the line. "One last thing. If you should be contacted by the media, would you avoid saying anything at all, as far as possible?"

"About the Blue project?"

"About anything."

He was gone. I put the phone down. I had an odd feeling that this whole conversation was not about Blue at all.

Blue and I had a session booked for the next day.

I congratulated him as we wrapped up. "That was great, I so get a feel for what it was like to be there. I'm sure this will come across brilliantly, just as it is."

"Great!"

"Actually . . ."

"Yes?"

"How do you feel about doing the next session right now, while we're on a roll? I can't wait to hear more and sometimes it's really worthwhile catching the mood. Do you have time?"

"Sure. That last section was fast, anyway, huh?"

"Yeah, we're getting a rhythm. I'll keep the tape rolling. The next topic I have is your first international tour – that work for you?"

"Yeah, sure. Wow, it was a blast, and I met some of my childhood idols . . ."

I had no trouble convincing Blue to talk again the next day, and by Wednesday I had the full 12 interviews ready for Kent.

"Do you want me to get the last transcripts done?"

"Leave it with me. We're going to get this into editing as soon as possible."

"When do I meet the editor?"

"I'm sorry?"

"I assumed you'd want me to work with the editor, clarifying anything they need. My contract said . . ."

"Oh, I'm sure they'll be able to get by. No need."

"Kent, you've already paid me, it's part of the service. If my name's going to be on the book I want to do everything I can to make it great."

"Really, no need. Just get the disk over here as soon as possible." His voice was almost sharp; then he softened it, "I'll call you if they have any questions."

I opened my mouth to protest again, but again the disconnecting click came without warning.

The polished receptionist had been replaced with another very similar – or perhaps she had simply dyed her hair and changed her makeup.

"The Blue King interviews for Kent." I handed the package across. "Is he here? Tasha Stuart."

Her eyes flickered to the closed door to her right and back to me. "He's out at an appointment. Was he expecting you?"

"Yes – well, more the disk. He didn't say he wanted to speak to me."

"Shall I get him to call you?"

"No, no need."

My feet dragged slightly as I left the building, as if I was walking in the wrong direction.

41

At a loose end I dropped by the café. The sign on the door showed the boys were in residence, but I could hear them, anyway.

The Lilac tour was getting near and Scott, Steven and Bernard were in an intense discussion.

"I think we can do this segue better. Steve, try the bass line with a syncopated rhythm, and Bern, pause for a beat or two, then come back on the off beat."

Steven played a few notes. "Like this?"

"Here, let me."

Steven pulled the strap of the bass over his head and watched intently as Scott put one foot up on an amplifier and balanced the bass guitar in front of his lead guitar. The sequence of notes sounded almost the same to me.

"Bern . . ." Bernard came in with the last line of the melody which died away into a series of chords, speeding up and changing key. Scott put up a finger, Bernard paused, Scott continued with his rhythm then motioned with his head for Bernard to come back in. All three nodded. Steven took back his bass and they went through the sequence again. The song changed into another, and as soon as it was underway Scott stopped playing. Bernard and Steven followed suit.

"That's great guys, really polished!"

I walked over to where Kate was sitting, an array of paper before her – album artwork, I saw, when I looked closer.

"Hey Tash! You've met Mike. He's a graphic designer, he's done some covers for us. What do you think?"

I think Mike's in love with you, was the first thought that came to mind. Mike was an old boyfriend. She keeps an army of them which reads like a trade directory: plumbers and electricians and decorators. I hadn't realised Mike was a designer, but it figured. I turned my attention to the pictures.

There were six different designs, all very different, from abstract to a flat photograph of the guys, not smiling, standing shoulder to shoulder. That one had a retro feel to it, reminded me of the Beatles. There was an arty photograph, if I were to title it, it would be "Band out of focus," but it was kind of cool, too. One of the abstracts looked like it was splattered with blood.

"Bernard likes that one," Kate said as I picked it up.

"Oh, please!" I said, tactlessly, just as Mike said "Me, too."

"Sorry." I grimaced at him but he really wasn't looking at me.

Had Kate dressed up just to torment him? If anything she was thinner than before and her top was sheer with a wide, deep V which skimmed across her black, minimal bra.

"Don't you get cold, with all that on display?" I should have stopped myself, but I was feeling oddly rattled.

Mike smirked. Kate laughed coolly. "Wake up in a good mood, did we? Anyway, what do you mean, 'all that'? When the band starts making money I'm going to get a boob job."

I rolled my head back and made an involuntary sound in the back of my jaw. When I gathered myself again I saw Mike nodding, with a big grin.

"Great of you to do these, Mike, it looks like a lot of work." God, I can be such a bitch, but he didn't catch my sarcasm, just nodded.

"Anything for Kate, huh?"

He nodded again.

Kate shot me a warning look. "Unless you're going to be helpful, you can go away. The recordings are done, so as soon as we've chosen a cover we can go into production. Now, seriously, what do you think?"

I looked at them again, eyes flipping from one to another. I picked up the Beatles one. "This."

"You don't like this one?" Kate pointed to the fuzzy black and white.

"Yeah, but it looks like something out of a café cookbook, I don't think it's your market."

She nodded. "Yeah, I get you."

She twisted around to where Mike was looking over her shoulder, alternating between his pictures and the front of her blouse.

"Is this your kind of music?" she gestured to the stage.

"I like it, yeah. Although I usually go for something a little bit heavier."

"And you like this one." She held up the streaks of blood, mouth twitching to one side. Mike shrugged an apology.

"What about Scott, Steven?"

"Scott likes the same one you do, and Steven says he doesn't care, just get it done so we can start selling it. So, what do you think, money bags? It's your call, really."

I stepped back. "No, no it isn't. You're the manager, you decide."

She took the picture out of my hand. "I like this one, too, and Scott has a pretty good marketing eye. Let's go with it. Mike, can you email the jpeg to the CD company? I want them to get on it this afternoon."

Mike nodded, collected the pile and reluctantly headed for the door.

"Come back any time." Kate flashed a smile that made Mike stumble in the doorway.

"What I can't understand is, why the room isn't full of your guys. What's to stop him taking up your invitation and moving in?"

She shrugged. "It's a subtle thing. Men are sensitive to the suggestion that they bore you, a couple of languid sighs is usually enough. And if not, Bernard just stands closer and closer to them till they take fright."

I laughed despite my disapproval. "You amaze me. How do you even come up with an answer to that question? It's like you've thought it all out!"

"Of course I have! God, how did we end up so different?"

"Who cares, I'm only glad we did."

She punched me, and I punched her back, then we stood, shoulders touching, watching the band play.

"I wish I understood you better."

She turned to me in surprise. "What's not to get?"

"The way you are with guys, for instance. You are so in control, all the time. Didn't a guy ever get under your skin?"

A troubled look crossed her eye. She looked back at the stage, at Bernard. Five seconds passed. I thought she wasn't going to answer, but then she took my arm and steered me towards the door. "Let's walk."

We crossed the road and followed the path along the river. Tourists were boarding a punt, full of the thrill of domestic adventure. I saw a familiar frown of frustration on Kate's face, like she has when I'm being timid.

"I so envy your courage." The words were out before I knew they were coming.

"Who, me? You're the brave one! The one with the real life, the home, the husband, the job."

"There's nothing brave about any of that, it just happens."

"It hasn't happened to me." She paused and stared into the river. Minutes passed. I bit my tongue and waited. "Did a guy ever get under my skin? Yeah. There was a guy, the two years before I came home."

"Two years?" I'd never seen her last six months with anyone.

She flicked her head around and turned her back, masking the movement by walking to a park bench and sitting down. She looked at the ground, a sheet of blonde hair hiding her face.

"I've never had that before, the desire to give more than I received." Her right shoulder twitched upwards. "This guy was rich, amazingly clever, a Cambridge Academic Fellow. Ancient family who I never met. I never met anyone in his life, we just had this private world in his college rooms. Of course, everybody must have known, it's such a concentrated place, but no-one met my eye as I came and went. Everything so discrete." Another long pause. "But the joy that was in those rooms, it made everything else fade into pallor. I lost track of everything else. I was working in a pub, that's where we met, but as I fell into the relationship I stopped noticing anything else. I went to work but I honestly can't remember anything that happened there. I had my room above the pub, but once I met him I wasn't really alive there any more, only when I was with him." Rapture and grief mixed in her face.

I couldn't hold myself in any longer. "So what happened?"

"I got pregnant. You know they said I'd never be able to. I was deliriously happy. So was Daniel. But then I had a miscarriage. I couldn't talk to him about it. So I came home."

I felt a slow whoosh and a thud at this sudden ending. "But you were so . . ." I remembered her entrance with the Adonis, how carefree and magical she seemed.

"I was only what I knew how to be. I can't think about this, Tasha, even now."

"But Kate, you have to. You have to grieve."

"I can't, Tash. I'm so afraid I'll lose myself completely."

I couldn't push her. I've never seen such anguish on a human face. "But what did you tell him?"

"He was there when it happened, he took me to the doctor. He wanted to take me back to his place but I made him drop me at work. He'll know why I went. He'll know."

"But . . . your heart . . . your heart's still there. I can see it." I put my hand out to her and she leaned into me; for one brief, deep second she let me in.

"I need to keep myself busy, Tash, it's the only way I'll get through."

42

The guys were gone when we got back to the café. I took Kate home on the back of my moped then rode slowly on to my place.

Steven was emptying the pantry of everything from fruit to tinned spaghetti.

"What's up?"

"I just forget to eat while we're rehearsing." His eyes were shining. "It's completely absorbing."

I hugged him as he wolfed down pears straight from a tin. "Can you get some fruit if you go to the supermarket tomorrow? I'm getting short on vitamins." He could hardly speak around his crammed mouth.

"Sure. Hey, we finished the Blue interviews this morning."

"Great! Are you happy?"

"Yeah, sure."

"You're not?"

"Yeah, I am. It's just . . ." I couldn't say anything about Kate. I looked back earlier in my day for something to tell him. "There's something funny with Kent."

"He doesn't like them?"

"I'm sure he'll be fine with them. It's not that, just, there was something he wasn't saying. And there was a rush at the last minute, when there wasn't before." I shook myself. "No point worrying, I've been trying to figure it out all day, time to forget it."

Steven had already moved on. "Hey, I'm still starving, want anything from McDonald's Drive Thru? I'll get dinner for the kids as well."

"Nah, I'll have some toast then go do some work. Tomorrow is the first day of the insurance interviews, I need to prepare."

My night was fragmented. First I couldn't get to sleep, echoes of Kate's face flashing between me and my dreams, and Kent's receptionist flickering occasionally in the mix – why wouldn't he see me? Then the phone rang, a wrong number, but after stumbling to the phone at 1:30 the adrenaline kept me awake another hour. At 4 I woke with a jolt, my elbow hitting Steven in the face.

"What?" he asked, sitting upright, too.

"Winnie. It's something about Winnie, I'm sure."

"Winnie," Steven repeated and dropped back onto his pillow. I was still awake half an hour later and gave up, went downstairs, made a strong coffee and started my day.

We filmed the insurance interviews in a stark white office but Al had brought in a tradesman's spotlight and a painting of his wife's to create the mood. The subject would sit in a small arm chair and I would sit just to the left of the camera, so when they faced me the angle would be good. Al was eager to play guinea pig.

"When we do the others I'll work the camera, but for mine, just press this button would you? Now for the one take wonder. Are you ready?"

I read my prepared introduction with warm, professional enthusiasm. This was like breathing to me now, very easy and natural. I made eye contact with Al and nodded encouragingly, at the start and periodically as he spoke. In early interviews I had done the habitual thing of speaking my confirmation, as one does in conversation – 'yes' and 'aha' – I had quickly learned to stop that habit, it sounded weird on the recordings. To replace it I used this definite nod, so the speaker stayed warm. People need feedback or they think you're not interested.

Al got more relaxed and more animated as the three minutes went by. By the end I was ready to buy some insurance from him myself.

"Fantastic!" I pressed the stop button and Al disconnected the microphone from his shirt.

"Yeah, wasn't it! Let's take a look."

The lighting needed some adjustment but otherwise it was really good. I took a deep breath of satisfaction. We were started, and it was going to be fine.

We had half an hour until the troops started arriving, at half hour intervals to allow for retakes and nerve calming. Al called for coffee and I asked him about himself, part of keeping myself on task, focused on the client, making them feel like a star. I love the way people warm and blossom with this kind of attention. It renews my faith in the world.

43

I was just icing Erica's birthday cake when she came out dressed for the party, in the backless top Kate had given her. What was I going to do? It was her birthday.

"Erica, please, won't you put something else on?"

"I like this. We're going to be dancing."

"Aren't you cold?"

"Mum, you are so transparent. What's wrong with it?"

"I've told you, it's a grownup style, it doesn't look right on an eight year old."

"I'm nine."

"Whatever."

Erica rolled her eyes.

"Please? What will the other mothers say?"

"Mum, you always say we should be our own person, not just follow the pack. You shouldn't care what they say."

There was no answer to that. Served me right for being so weak in the first place.

"Besides, Mum, I won't be the only one dressed up. You wait. You should have seen them at the disco."

She was right. I felt like a giant in a music video. Erica's friends' clothes were sleeveless, low cut, crop cut, with torn jeans or mini skirts. The only child properly dressed looked like a poor relative from the country, totally out of place and embarrassed. Thank goodness Erica had asked to have a dance party at home rather than go to the movies as I had suggested. I'd have been lucky if one of these teenyboppers hadn't been abducted.

"I still disapprove," I said sulkily to Erica once her friends had gone.

"I know, Mum. But you've got to go with the times. Here, have a chocolate, I've got loads."

I still hadn't had any feedback from Kent about the Blue recordings, and although I told myself not to worry it was like trying to ignore someone crocheting the hair at the back of my head.

Wanting quiet after the party I retreated to my office to do some editing. Calmed by the process as ever, when I finished the job half an hour later I was ready to go back into company again.

"Who's hungry?"

The three girls looked at me with guilty faces and I saw several plates of party leftovers, plastic wrap pushed aside, empty. Steven was sitting on the sofa reading a magazine, oblivious.

"Okay, why don't you guys go outside and run some of that off. I'll just make dinner for Dad and me, you can have a sandwich later if you want."

Steven just grunted when I asked him what he fancied for dinner, so I wandered into the kitchen looking for inspiration. I'm not the most confident or interested cook - Steven is far more proficient. But I have a couple of old favourites. I looked through the drawer for the cookbook I wanted and finally found it on the bottom shelf of the pantry, under a bag of flour. Our kitchen is tiny, the cookbooks always have to balance somewhere precarious. As I assembled the ingredients I thought how much easier it would be to have audio recipes on my iPod, they'd be right there when I needed them, in my pocket so they wouldn't get spotted with food and I wouldn't have to keep turning around to see the book, or skim through to find my place - I'd just pause at each instruction then start it again when I was ready.

I assembled the base of the spinach pie and put it in the oven, got the frozen spinach out of the freezer and put it in the microwave to steam. It was while I was whisking the eggs that my movement slowed and stopped. Audio recipes. Was anyone else doing it?

The idea played around and around my mind as I filled the pie on auto pilot and put it back in the oven to cook. Why not? Some people wouldn't go for it, but some would. The Internet possibilities were huge, too, I knew there were lots of recipes on the Internet but no way of charging for them. What if there was a description of the dish and the ingredients, then you could download the audio track for a small fee?

Already I was rehearsing my sales pitch to a publisher's cookbook editor.

"It's ideal - recipes are an information product, and one where the passion of the voice would add huge value. Imagine the chef describing the dish in that fabulous way they do when in their mind they are right there eating it. They could give short anecdotes of summer lunches under trees or eating in front of the fire on a cold winter night. No-one else is doing it, it would be a great gift idea for Christmas sales."

I knew better than to throw an undeveloped idea at Steven, especially while he was eating. I couldn't wait for tomorrow when I could make some calls. It would be a fun break from the standard marketing calls I still made every day.

44

"Rebecca Hancroft."

"Hi, I'm Tasha Stuart. Am I speaking to the cookbook editor?"

"Cuisine editor, that's right."

"I'm a professional interviewer specialising in profile interviews for professional and creative people. Most of my work is about interviewing people to bring out the best in them, bring out their passion and their story. I've done a number of interviews with chefs for restaurant websites."

"Yes?"

"I've had an idea about an audio version of a cookbook. I wondered if you might be interested in discussing it."

"Possibly . . . tell me more."

I took a deep breath. No matter how many of these big, brave calls I made, my heart still pounded in my chest. I exhaled, trying to steady my breathing and my voice.

"I was thinking of recording recipes so that people can cook using an iPod rather than a book. There are lots of advantages – easy to find, audio so you can keep your eyes on your work. And getting to hear the voice of the chef, their passion and enthusiasm. They might even give more detailed instructions of what each step is supposed to look like . . ."

"What about the pictures, though, food is a very visual thing, people want to see what they are making, it helps them decide."

"Yes, that's true, particularly for highly visual people. But others are more auditory, or would just find this more convenient. You might even double up sales, where people have the book, know they like the recipes and would use this as an easy reminder when they're making an old favourite."

"Well, I'm not sure. I don't see it myself, but feel free to send me a proposal, I'll talk to our editorial committee about it."

Okay. A cold fish. So I needed another access.

"I'll do that. I have your email address here from your website. Would you mind if I contact a couple of your writers, also, to see if they would be interested?"

There was a hesitation. I suspected she wanted to say no, but what reason could she give? "As long as you make it clear there is no promise at this stage."

"Of course. Thanks for your time. Have a great day!"

"Pah!"

"What?" Kate turned from the other desk where she was working on a list of businesses from the Internet. Even though the album was finished we had got into a routine of working together for a couple of hours most mornings. I paid her commission on the work she generated.

"Closed-minded witch."

"So she said no. Onwards and upwards."

"She didn't say no, she was just a witch."

"Not the first and not the last. So what now?"

"She asked for a proposal. But I think I'll talk to one of her writers first, get some enthusiasm going from that direction if I can, then I can write that into the proposal and maybe even ask them to go to bat for the idea. I think it could be the start of something big. People said nobody would ever watch TV, they'd rather keep listening to the radio. I think this could be like that!"

"And no delusions of grandeur or anything?"

"Shut up."

I had a chef in mind, high profile, one of the bestsellers on the Whitcoulls' website. She was the reason I had started with this particular publisher. I did a web search and found she had a website of her own: email address, phone number, everything.

"Here I go."

The phone seemed to ring forever, and then I heard a cheerful voice on the other end. "Hi, Anthea speaking."

I had to stop myself exclaiming that I hadn't expected to get her straight away. "Hi, I'm Tasha Stuart . . ."

"Tasha Stuart! You did that interview with the girl criminal!"

I had trained myself not to categorise Winnie that way, but I wasn't going to correct her.

"Yes, that's me . . ."

"Wow! That interview was brilliant – she's quite a little actress, isn't she, knows how to create the impression she wants. I had so much fun the next day wondering what it was she wasn't saying."

Again I wasn't going to disagree, but this was a different view than I'd heard from anyone else.

"I'm phoning because I've had an idea I wanted to talk to you about."

"What is it?" her voice was eager and excited, flattering.

"Audio cookbooks – taking your books and recording them so people can cook using iPods."

There was a moment's silence, then "Wow! Great idea! I've never seen anyone else do that."

"I've talked to Rebecca at Callum Press. She asked me to send in a proposal and she'd take it to the editorial committee."

"Yeah, right. That'll happen."

Her scepticism chilled me. "You don't think it will."

"Not that way. Rebecca's fine if you do things the way she knows works, but anything new . . ."

I found myself shaking my head in tune with her words. "So what do you suggest?"

"Oh, do the proposal, it's just it won't work on its own. I say we just start. Record it. Then I'll take it to them with the proposal myself."

It sounded like great news, on the surface, but what if they didn't like it? The publisher would have copyright, we couldn't just take the recordings somewhere else to sell.

"What if they don't buy?"

"They will."

Was it worth the risk? "Fantastic. Only . . ."

"Yeah?"

"It's just, usually if I do a speculative job, we have a contract, a profit share, and it's . . ."

"Tell you what, I'll cover your costs. You can invoice me and if it doesn't work out, I'll pay you. But if we can work a royalty split with the publisher, we'll throw away that invoice. How much do you think?"

I did some quick calculations. How long might it take to record one recipe? Maybe 15 minutes with ingredients and a bit of back story. "How many recipes?"

"In the last book? 54."

"So I'm guessing about 20 hours of recording time, then editing. But the editing of most of it can wait until we've got the go ahead. I'm thinking aloud."

"You go right ahead."

I did some rapid calculations. "At full rate it would be somewhere around $9000 for the completed job, less if we don't do all the editing . . . But to just pay my costs, with the chance of a real deal once we're done . . . If you could cover an invoice for $1800, then we're set."

"No problem."

"Really?"

"Really."

"And you live in Auckland."

"Yeah. Where are you?"

"Christchurch. But I'm coming up next week to do a couple of days of interviews, I could stay on."

"Fab! You can stay with me."

"Really?"

"Sure – comfortable bed, respectable meals. I'm not a bad cook."

I hesitated. "Are you really sure?"

"Sure I'm sure, they let me write recipe books."

"I mean . . ."

She had a wild, beautiful laugh. "I know what you meant. I'm just teasing. Listen, if we don't get on it's not going to work anyway, I'll just send you home."

"It's a deal."

45

This was the longest I had left my family, ever. I clung to the girls when Steven took them to school, way more for my sake than theirs.

"I'll miss you."

"That's okay, Mummy. We'll call you every night."

"Thanks, Hon. I'll be back next week and then we've got the Lilac concert."

"Sure, Mum." Greta patted my hand. "You'll be fine. Here, take Herman. You can hide him in your handbag."

Sitting in the airport departure lounge I took Herman out and put him on my knee. He was small and brown and very scruffy, Greta's favourite bear when she was about 4. I hugged him tight.

Al met me at the airport and we drove straight to the insurance office. We had five hours of interviews scheduled for the afternoon, and the same tomorrow, cut back to 20 minutes per slot now we were practiced. "I'm all set up, so we can get straight into it. These guys don't mess about. Are you flying back tomorrow night?"

I explained the Anthea project.

"Cool! I have her book myself. I'm a big fan. I was going to suggest since we're both out of town we have dinner tonight. Do you think she'd join us?"

I had a bizarre, tiny flicker of nerves at the thought of dinner alone with Al. What was I thinking? He had always been a perfect gentleman. It's just it seemed a little intimate.

"I'll ask her," I said, taking my mobile phone from my pocket.

Anthea was keen. "She wants to know where to meet us."

"Get her to recommend a good restaurant close to her home, and tell her I'm buying. Find out her address and say we'll pick her up at 8."

I find that even in semi-social situations it's simpler to retain the professional client relationship. I usually try to sit back and let them do most of the talking, it makes things easier to manage and people love a good listener.

Anthea wasn't having any of that, though. She was full of questions from the first moment, screaming with pleasure when we met and delighted to meet Al as well.

"So what are you doing for Al's company?"

I deferred to Al to tell the story, but Anthea kept coming back to me. With a glass of wine and Anthea's encouragement, I found myself in a double act with Al describing the humorous moments of the afternoon.

Anthea was also fascinated with the subject of Winnie, drawing Al into her interest also.

"What was she like when she wasn't on camera? She was so polished on screen."

"Not too much different. Very poised."

"And do you really think she was telling the truth? Has she really cleaned up her organisation, shut it down?"

The question took me by surprise. "It's my job to bring out the best in my clients, to present their best face to the world. I guess I'd find it . . . disloyal . . . unethical, to question . . ."

"But surely you must have wondered. I couldn't stop myself. I'd be asking all sorts of inappropriate questions."

I looked down at my hands. I could feel Al's quiet eyes on me, as well as Anthea's eager ones.

"Like I said, she's my client, it's a professional relationship."

"But what if she is guilty? How would you feel that you helped her cover it up?"

"I don't think it's a possibility," I snapped.

Anthea laughed. "Sorry. I know I'm impertinent. Just tell me to take a jump. Shall we order dessert?"

TASHA STUART INTERVIEWS . . .

46

I wanted a break after the second session of Al's interviews, before finding Anthea again. She was lots of fun but I needed some solitude. Al dropped me back at the hotel on his way to the airport, surprising me by kissing my cheek as he departed.

"Fantastic work! We make a great team. Have a look at our website tomorrow, I'll try to get some of those interviews live this evening."

"Thanks for everything, Al. Enjoy your flight."

I paused in the lobby before collecting my bag from the concierge. This was as good as anywhere for a quiet drink and some thinking time.

I checked my phone. A message from Kate saying she had some good news. She would wait. A text from Steven saying he was thinking of me. That made me smile, he must be missing me. I left the phone on silent and wandered into the empty bar. A waitress was polishing glasses. "L&P? No ice."

"Sure, I'll bring it over."

The hotel was on the side of a steep hill and the terrace of the bar looked out over a wide residential valley, some grand old houses on the lower slopes and modern townhouses above. I took a long breath through my nose and propped my chin on my hands. My eyes closed. I realised that for the past few hours I had completely lost myself.

The two days of interviews had been a bit of a marathon. Back to back, churning through, connecting with fifteen people one after another and no breaks in between, then starting again this morning. I was exhausted. I could put my head down on the table right here and go to sleep.

There was an element of culture shock, too. Aucklanders are straight to the point compared with Christchurch people, say what they think without any padding. My ego had taken a couple of knocks which I hadn't had time to process, just kept going, the consummate professional. It would be nice to indulge in a little self-pity now, but I'd hardly begun when a receptionist came through with a cordless phone. It was Kent.

"Tasha!" there was huge relief in Kent's voice, and something else, too, "I'm glad I caught you."

"Kent, what is it? Some problem with the recordings?"

"Recordings?" He sounded very vague, as if he hadn't a clue what I was talking about.

"Blue King."

"Oh! No, nothing to do with that. There's something breaking, about Winnie. The press will come looking for you. Is there somewhere you can go? It will be so much better if you don't have to say anything. Can you go to ground?"

Go to ground? I had the urge to laugh. He was starting to sound like a spy. "I'm staying with . . . a friend, tonight. For a few days. I'll lay low."

"Good. Good. And for God's sake, turn your phone on, I was worried I'd never find you. But don't answer it unless you recognise the number."

There was a click and he was gone.

I took my phone out again. After the morning session I had transferred my office number to my mobile. I looked at it now. Ten missed calls, six of them from Kent. Messages from two reporters. What the hell was happening? I called the call diversion number and put the calls back to my answering service. I hoped to goodness the operators would have the sense not to be drawn into any questions. Most of them knew nothing about me, just worked from a very simple script. I considered calling to let the supervisor know, but before I could dial, the still silent phone registered a call. Home.

It was Kate. "God, Tasha, what's happening? The home phone is running hot. People asking if you knew anything about that kidnapping."

"What kidnapping?"

"That politician, last June."

"Me, why should I know anything about that?" And then the bottom dropped out. That was the day I was with Winnie, waiting for her migraine to clear. He had been kidnapped from Nelson airport, the same day we were there. "Oh fuck."

"Tasha?"

"I don't know anything. But I have a very bad feeling. Winnie. Kate, I have to go. Take the phone off the hook, and don't say anything to anyone. Can you take the girls back to your place when you pick them up? And call Al to postpone the Wellington interviews, just in case."

"Sure. Will you come home?"

"I think I'd better not. No-one knows where I am here. Sorry to leave you in a mess."

223

"No sweat. You take care."

I turned on the ringer and kept the phone in my hand. What now? The only thing I could think was Anthea. I had her mobile number.

"I think you were right."

"Tasha?"

"Something is blowing up with Winnie. Where are you? Can I come to your place now?"

"I'm doing a cooking demonstration at 3, be about an hour. Can you wait till then?"

"Sure, I'll take a walk. Call me when you're free?"

I was about to leave the hotel when I remembered my bag. It had wheels but I still felt conspicuous wandering the streets with it. I found a park bench tucked away in some lush green plants growing by a quiet roadside. My instinct was to hide myself away.

47

We watched the coverage on the 6 o'clock news, then changed the channel for the 6:30. Winnie was being questioned about the kidnap of the politician, who it turned out had been on my flight. They didn't have much more information than that, so mostly what they did was show pictures of her book, describe it in unflattering terms - "Creative extension of the truth" "Web spun by a criminal genius" - and show excerpts from our TV interview. There I sat, nodding and sympathetic, looking either complicit or a total idiot. I didn't like either option.

Anthea was enjoying the whole situation. I just felt sick.

Her children and husband alternately looked at the screen and regarded me with curiosity. I receded into the open plan kitchen, turning my face away. As the next item came on Anthea switched off the set and shooed them out. "Let Tasha breathe. I'll come up and do stories later."

"No problem, I'll do it."

"Thanks, Hon."

She closed the door behind them and turned to watch me. She fetched my untouched dinner plate from where I'd left it on the coffee table and put it down on the kitchen counter. "Come on, eat something."

It looked delicious, fresh and colourful just like the covers of her books. I couldn't eat a bite. I stared at the glass of white wine in my hand. I was either going to drink it all in one gulp or not touch it at all. Anthea watched delightedly as I threw the whole thing down.

"Another?" She leaned the bottle towards my glass hopefully.

I shook my head.

"Come on, cheer up! You haven't committed any crime, this will blow over."

Many possible responses swirled in my head, about my career, my future, what people would think. All faint-hearted stuff.

"I've never been in trouble before. I never even had a detention at school. It's not fair."

I stared at the black granite counter, tipping my glass from one side to the other. Finally Anthea took it from me.

"Listen, look at me. That stuff you said last night, about responsibility to your client. Can you really say you had no idea? Or did you really know, and not admit it? Who are you going to blame?"

The world was grey as self-realisation sank excruciatingly through my whole frame. I stared into her eyes, a mirror for my guilt. She stared back frankly.

"So. Come on. There's no good moping about, and there's nothing you can do tonight." She picked up the bottle and her glass. "Let's go and start these recordings."

"No, I can't, I really can't. I think I should just go to bed, if you don't mind."

"Yeah, like you could sleep right now! What was that you said last night, about the consummate professional? About knowing how to turn on your professional enthusiasm on call, at any moment?"

"I know. But this time I really can't."

"Oh yes, you can. Come on!"

With my direction Anthea found the voice recorder in my bag and brought a copy of her book through to a small office at the back of the house. "It's pretty quiet in here. Will it do?"

I took a look around with a practiced eye, listened for background noise with a practiced ear. "Yes, this will be fine."

Anthea started rummaging for the microphones, taking out the smooth black cases and opening one. "Here, let me." I hurriedly reached out before she tangled the delicate wire. She sat back with a smug expression while I set things up. I felt myself grow automatically calmer and more optimistic as I followed this familiar routine.

I took out the notepad where I had written my thoughts about the format.

> Title of the dish first
>
> Ingredients
>
> Anecdote/rave about taste
>
> Method of preparation

I showed it to her. "What do you think?"

She nodded, looks good. "Why have you got the ingredients before the rave? In the book I do it the other way around."

"When people look at a book they can see the whole page at once, look at what they want to. When they listen they'll often need to know they have the ingredients before they choose a recipe – especially if they want to cook from what they have. I'm just talking about a quick list."

Anthea nodded.

"Anyway, we'll get feedback. We can always do it different for the next book if people want it. Are you ready? What do you want to do first."

It was magic the way the time flew. Listening to Anthea talk about food was a deeply sensual experience, her passion came through in the texture of her voice, the way she varied pace to convey the stretch of a dough or the final seasoning of the dish. The step-by-step methods, especially, came alive in her phrasing, I could see and smell each progression along the way. She was fast, too, very few mistakes. Editing would be quick. "I'm so used to talking while I cook," she explained. "Like the demonstration I did today. So it's easy."

In two hours we had recorded 12 recipes. "This is going to go fast! We might be able to get it done in a couple of days now." I reached in my bag for my phone, silent again for the recording. 28 missed calls.

"Do you mind if I just phone Steven?"

Anthea discretely left the room.

48

We didn't have much to say to each other.

"I'm sorry. Sorry you've had to go through this. Sorry I'm not there. Do you want me to come home?'

"That would just make it worse. Are you getting anything done?"

"Yeah, faster than I thought. I could come back on Thursday, probably."

"We'll see how things are. Kent called, by the way. He wants you to call."

"Yeah, I know, six missed calls. I'll talk to him once I say goodnight to the girls. Anything else we need to talk about first?"

There was a silence. Steven's voice was very quiet. "Did you know?"

"No! Of course not!" I didn't say it, but my head was screaming 'Even you?'

"Okay. Here's Greta."

My hand was shaking after I hung up. Charlotte concerned, Erica loving the excitement, Greta a little bit scared and pleased she had given me Herman. And Steven doubting.

I took a deep breath and dialled Kent.

"Ah Tasha, finally."

"I was recording."

"I wanted to warn you. I think the media will soon make the connection that you were on the flight. At the moment all the attention on you is because of the interviews. But once they do, they'll start asking if you were more closely involved."

"Kent, was he there? At the house? When we were?"

"He was in the helicopter, in the car and in the house."

My stomach cart-wheeled. "How?"

There was a pause. "Drugged, in a sports bag."

"How much do the police know?"

"They know all that."

"But they don't know we were in the car, and at the house."

"No. But in your case I'm pretty sure they'll work it out."

"In my case?"

"It's there on the recording. Winnie refers to her birthday in 7 days time. That dates your interview exactly. They will work out you were there."

I realised what he was saying. When they did he wouldn't be coming forward to keep me company.

"I can't lie to the police for you, Kent."

"I know, my dear. But perhaps for old times' sake you could avoid volunteering information if they don't ask for it."

I nodded. "What else do you know?"

I sensed he was considering his answer. "It was an accident. It wasn't supposed to happen as it did. Yes, your visit was a cover for meeting that plane. They just wanted his suitcase, some papers he was carrying, hoping he would blame the airline, but something went wrong. He was knocked out fighting to get it back and Ham panicked, put him in the car in Nelson. Then he phoned Winnie to ask for instructions. That's when she made the change of plan.

"They spirited you away to your room but I overheard them talking. Winnie trusts me. When she realised I knew she asked for help. The situation was too big for her. It was me who suggested just returning him, as simply and quickly as possible, case and all. There were a couple of sticky moments. But in the end she did as I suggested, as I'm sure you know by now. He was gone by the time you were let out of your room in the morning."

"So what's her story if she doesn't mention you."

"It will be better for her if it appears she made that decision alone. Which she did in the end, actually. But the public will be more sympathetic if they don't know she struggled with it."

"More spin, Kent, even now?"

"Always. Good night, my dear. Thank you in advance for your discretion."

Well, fine. But I knew pretty well exactly how far that discretion would go.

49

Kent was right. By Sunday afternoon the news was out that our audio interview was filmed the same day. "Was Tasha Stuart in on kidnapping?" was the new headline. Half an hour later Steven called to say the police were on their way.

I had time to pack my bag with shaking hands. I hugged Anthea, thanking her over and over for keeping me safe and occupied for the past two days.

"You bet! It's been fun."

Last thing I took my recorder from her desk and put it back in my bag. I had backed up the files onto her computer. My dim, fearful view of police questioning vaguely included destruction or loss of property, and I wanted those recipes safe.

There was a knock at the door.

"That'll be for me," I said, my voice suitably and naturally dramatic. Anthea laughed out loud.

I was terrified. Unnecessary movement in my body ceased. I noticed my eyes searching the blank room while my head stayed absolutely still. The detective was polite, softly spoken. I answered every question with way more information than was called for. Kent's name slipped out before I had been there three minutes as I recounted every detail of the arrangements and the flights.

Winnie had already told them she had arranged for me to be on that particular flight and why. I spilled every detail, far more than I thought I remembered. I knew the colour of the suit of the woman sitting on the other side of Kent, I knew which row the politician had been sitting in even though I didn't consciously remember passing him when we boarded. I vividly described how nervous I was about the interview. "It was supposed to be in Nelson. I thought it would be in Nelson. I had never done an author interview before, I was just starting out, I'd only done a few business coaches and chefs and people like that, you know, short pieces for their websites, what sort of food they cooked, how they enjoyed food etc. This opportunity was out of the blue. Kent said they chose me because of my sympathy with my subjects but I realise now that was a mistake, a really big mistake, I should have known she was lying, that she was just using me to project a certain image so she could continue with her deplorable lifestyle. I feel such a dupe, such a fool. I'm so sorry. What can I do to make up for it? I'm so sorry."

The detective looked slightly sceptical as I dissolved into hysterics but after a while a look of concern crossed his face. He told me to get up off the floor but I literally couldn't.

"Wait here." The door locked behind him and I felt my sobs slow. He returned with a cup of tea and held out a hand to me. I stared at it several seconds before grasping it and pulling myself up. "I'll be back shortly," he said, but perhaps an hour passed before he returned. There were more questions.

No, I didn't see him being loaded into the first car, or the helicopter, or the second car, or taken into the house. I felt something heavy put into the boot at the airport but didn't think anything about it. No, I had no idea he was there. Yes, I understood the general nature of Winnie's business – I had begun reading her book – but there was no admission of crime. No, I was not surprised to be locked in my room, everything about the situation and the people was foreign to me. No, I did not realise it was unusual to be at the house until Kent said so on the way home.

"Leman was there at the house also."

Oops. Yes, Kent was there, too, he was her agent, he oversaw the interview.

"And he didn't tell you what was going on?"

"No, I didn't find out until after it was on the news earlier in the week. I knew about the kidnapping, from TV, but nothing else."

My speech was getting more regular now. I was finding my equilibrium.

"And you had no idea?"

"I was a fool, I know I was. Naïve. But no, I had no idea."

"Okay. Wait again, please."

"Just a moment."

"Yes?"

"I just remembered, I heard the helicopter fly out and back in the morning. Out at around 7 a.m. and back during the interview – we had to take a pause while it landed. I forgot. That must have been when they returned him."

"That's probably right. I'll be back shortly."

After a while I put my head on the desk. My cheeks were throbbing. When the door opened again it woke me.

"Okay, Tasha. We'll need to talk to you again in the morning but you can go for tonight. Let the desk know where you are staying. I believe your husband is here waiting for you."

"Steven?" For some reason this was the least believable part of the evening.

"Steven!" I screamed when I saw him. I ran to him and threw my arms around him. This was the kindest thing anyone has ever done for me.

If I'd had time to think I would have dreaded how he would look at me, how angry he would be, but he was just lovely.

"Come on. I've booked a motel just around the corner. They've given me your bag. Let's go."

50

I had forgotten that the Auckland Lilac concert was on Saturday. Bernard, Kate and Scott arrived on Friday morning and they all spent the day at the arena setting up, rehearsing, absorbing the atmosphere. They were all walking balls of adrenaline, hovering some centimetres above the floor. Having checked in with the police station in the morning, I was free to spend the afternoon and evening at the gig.

Wow, what a night! I got to be backstage, to watch the guys give the performance of their lives. Steven was almost throwing up but Kate took him aside and somehow put some steel into him. By the time they were announced he was pumped like I'd never seen him.

We all went out front to watch the main show, feel the energy reach a new level as Lilac came out on the stage. How can someone so small, someone you could pass in the street and think nothing more than "She's cool" fill such an enormous space? Tens of thousands of people were silent until she spoke, and then a great cheer went up, filling the sky. One guitar chord and that pregnant, empty moment erupted with music.

For 90 glorious minutes I forgot all my problems and fears. For that space of time I was myself again, confident and free.

"Detective Stone, when can I go home? I want to get back to my kids."

"I'll see what we can do. We appreciate your cooperation so far. I think we can wrap up everything we need from you this morning. You'll be available in Christchurch if we need you."

It was strange arriving home, greeting my children. I hugged them like I'd been away a month.

"Don't cry, Mum, we'll look after you." I put my hand on Greta's long, loose curls and started to cry again. I sat close to them all evening and cried again as I dropped them to school the next morning. I ignored the mothers' curious stares, taking Charlotte's scooter and riding home.

What was I going to do with my day? I had no heart for work. I'd have liked to go to the café but the guys were in Wellington, setting up for Tuesday's concert. We'd see them on Wednesday when they arrived for the concert here on Thursday night.

I decided to take a couple of days off, read, relax, recover. I was feeling pretty low when Detective Stone called on Thursday morning.

"Ms Stuart, are you free to come in today? There are a couple more things I'd like to get straight. I've been in Nelson, and I'm just here for the day."

"Will it take long, it's just . . ."

"As long as it takes," he snapped. "Sorry to be brusque, I'll do my best."

So it wasn't really a question, it was an order. "I'll be there in half an hour."

I was getting used to the routine by now. Sit in a room. Answer a few questions, mostly ones I thought I had answered before. Detective leaves the room and I'm left waiting. At 2:30 I started to get anxious. At three I called Kate and left a message, praying she could arrange to have the girls collected from school. She texted back and I relaxed a little. At five, with Detective Stone out of the room, I asked the sergeant for permission to leave, so I could get to the concert. Denied. By 6:30 when he returned I started begging and at 7 he sighed, said we were finished and let me go.

I still had time to get to the stadium, parking a kilometre away and running for it. I had my backstage pass from last Saturday in my bag. I hoped it would work.

The security guard looked at the pass, then at me. "No, no good, this is for Eden Park."

"Please! That's my husband's band, I missed them to get my backstage pass for here, I have to get in."

"You'll have to go round the front and buy a ticket."

"There, that guy knows me." I pointed to one of the roadies I had met in Auckland.

The guard raised an eyebrow. The roadie nodded briefly, too busy to stop. I could hear the band's first number starting.

"Okay, I can't let you backstage without a pass, but you can go through here, watch the show from out front."

I could have kissed him.

I pushed my way through a group of kids already dancing. Kate would be pleased, I thought, look at them getting the feel of the beat.

I waved at Steven but the lights were in his eyes. Even though he couldn't see me I relaxed, knowing I was in the right place. I scanned the crowd wondering where the girls were, wondering who would be with them when I didn't make it. Kate's text: "No worries, all sorted" didn't give me any clue.

One number followed another, in the "hit hard, back off, big finish" wave they had developed over countless gigs. It was so great to be here. For the forty five minutes they were playing I forgot everything, all the stress and turmoil of the last weeks, and of today.

They got to the last piece with a thunder of applause. I expected them to leave the stage, but instead, Bernard came out with a hand-held mic to speak.

"Thanks so much, Christchurch, Café Storm's home town!"

There was a cheer, spreading back through the audience as they gradually understood his words.

"And now, by special authorisation of Lilac herself, we have an incredible treat for you!" Another cheer. I had never seen this side of Bernard. He really had them. "To perform Lilac's multi-million-seller "So What?" my very beautiful nieces Greta, Erica and Char!"

My eyes opened wide. What was happening? The band played the opening sequence, the stage went dark and a few seconds later the lights were full on and there were my girls, singing and dancing with a wild joy I had never seen before. I watched them in awe, torn between chest-bursting pride in their performance and bad-mother horror at seeing them so vulnerably exposed in Kate's devil-worship backless tops. I could kill her, and Steven, and Bernard. And Scott, too. But look at them! Just look at them! Beautiful.

51

"Mum, Mum we were in the concert! Did you see?"

I had finally got hold of Kate and got access backstage. The girls were so explosive that I took them down the steps to let them leap and scream out of the way. I hugged them all tight, imperfectly holding back tears.

"Do you have jackets?" I turned as someone came down the stairs with jumpers for them all.

"You made it! I hoped you would."

"Steven, what . . ?"

"Tash, shh. I'll explain it all later. Let's take them out front and watch the show."

We were all still high the next morning. I made pancakes for breakfast but Erica and Greta could hardly eat, jumping up from the table every couple of minutes to act out a moment from the day before. Charlotte was humming, smiling, occasionally breaking into song. I was laughing when the phone rang. It was Blue King.

"Hey, Hon. I heard about your troubles."

It took me a few moments to change modes, move my voice into the right mood for this subject. "Thanks, Blue, you didn't have to call."

"Well, I did and I didn't. You know we're going to print with the book next week?"

"Yeah, I'm so excited, it's the biggest thrill of my career, having my name there with yours!" This felt better, more in tune with the mood of the house.

"That's what I wanted to talk to you about. Your name's not going to be on it."

My breath pulled to a sharp stop, I had to deliberately restart it to speak, catching it and coughing. "But, why?" And then it was all clear. Blue wanted to let people know he hadn't killed his friend, that it had been a drug overdose: tragic, but accidental. He was eloquent about it in the book, moving, convincing. And now I was way more famous than I'd ever dreamed of, for covering up a kidnapping. Not the best advocate. Still, a last piece of me kept fighting. "But Blue, the contract, it says I have a credit."

"Would you really ask for that, now?" he asked gently, and left a pause which I didn't fill. "I know what it means to you, Doll, Kent asked me to remind you about the 'bringing into disrepute clause' but I know I don't have to do that. You'll understand what we need to do."

"Kent!" Instant anger consumed my breath and all the power went from my voice. "It was Kent who . . ."

"Hold on, Tasha. Just remember who is responsible for what you do."

My anger ebbed away to be replaced by sadness.

"So are we good?"

"Yeah, Blue, we're good. Good luck with the book."

He hung up and I sank down onto the floor and began to cry.

52

I refused to get out of bed the next morning. "It's Saturday," I sulked, when Steven came to find out where I was. "I'm not moving."

I sensed him hovering by the bed for another minute, then heard the door close behind him. Good. I just wanted to wallow. I pulled the duvet over my head and worked up all the misery I could muster.

It wasn't fair! I worked so hard to build something up and I was really proud of what I had achieved. Good income, enough to feed and house us all. Great relationships with clients, and providing excellent value in the product. I recalled the testimonial I had got just two weeks before, saying my promotional interview had helped this client double his turnover. He was ecstatic. And now it was all falling around my ears. No-one would hire me ever again. From here on it was total failure all the way. I cried for a while, trying to ignore the fact that it was taking some effort to keep the tears coming.

Steven returned with coffee and croissants. This was the moment of choice. I could send him away, but that would tip me spiralling further and faster downwards. A few years ago that's what I would have done. This slide begun, it might be months before I took real joy in the world again. I peeked out from under the duvet at Steven standing there, brow creased with worry, and realised I couldn't be bothered with this mood any more. I sat up, took the tray onto my knee. "You're an angel. Sit with me?"

He perched tentatively on the edge of the bed. I made more room for him and encouraged him to relax. He watched me take a sip of coffee, cut my croissant and spread it with butter, with jam. He waited until I had had a bite or two, another sip of coffee.

"Honey, what did Blue King say last night?"

I put the croissant down, leaned back on my pillow, stared at the ceiling and inhaled and exhaled through my nose. I was surprised I had the courage to look back at Steven as I answered. "They're taking my name off his book. Because of . . ."

"The kidnapping."

Something about the rawness of the fact stated so baldly caught my sense of humour. I almost laughed. "I guess when you say it like that, it makes sense. Not, 'Tasha, you're just not good enough' or 'Tasha, we've decided not to use your stuff after all' but 'Tasha, you were involved in a kidnapping. Associating with you is bad for business.' "

Steven eyed me warily.

"I guess I don't need to take it personally." And then I did laugh, and Steven joined me. A moment later I sobered again. "I'm just not sure what it will mean for my career."

Steven took my hand. "Just forget about it today. It's the weekend. The girls would love to see you downstairs. An express letter came, from Lilac. Incredibly generous, she's paid them each $1,000. They are wild about it, want to go shopping. If you're up to it."

"Wow." The feeling was like warm food in a starving stomach. My face crumpled.

"Hey! What is it?"

"Nothing." I reached along his arm, wrapped my hand around his forearm, near his elbow. "Will you find me something to wear? I can't make any decisions this morning."

"Sure." He came back with jeans, boots, a cuddly sweater. Just what I needed.

"Tell the girls I'll be right down."

It was going to take months or longer for Winnie's case to come to trial. I felt sick for her. She was really only a child, less than four years older than Charlotte, after all. I'd have to give evidence, and that terrified me, but I tried to put my own feelings aside. I wished I could help her – maybe I could help bring out her intention to reform, the impossible dilemma of a daughter who so loved a father who was becoming incapacitated – but until the trial there was nothing I could do.

Blue's book came out, it was in all the bookshops. He sent me a copy, signed "Thanks for everything, you're my shining star, Blue." There was a cheque inside it, too, with a note. £5,000. This was the month for celebrity generosity! I called him to say thank you but just got his answer phone.

Work had slowed down a little. I didn't have the heart for making cold calls and asked Kate to take a break, too. "It's time for me to take stock. Decide what I really want."

I'd been in touch with Anthea, told her it would be a few more days before I got the proposal together for her publisher.

"Okay. Just send me the invoice. I want to pay it this week."

"But why? That was only if things didn't work out."

"Just a hunch. I think you may be going cold on the idea, and if you've been paid you'll have to keep things moving."

"I'm not going cold on it, I just . . ."

"Have no stomach for anything any more? Listen, I get it. You've been through the wringer. But get over it. The sooner you build your momentum again the better you'll feel. Go talk to someone. Then get moving."

Talk to someone. Who? Wendy!

"Finally, back from the dead. I thought I must have been moved to the other list."

Wendy often teases me about the fact that a couple of years ago I made a list of people I would bother keeping up with. She was on it. There were only three other names.

"I've been kind of . . . elsewhere. Got time for coffee?"

"Let's make it a walk. I could use some fresh air."

We met in Little Hagley Park and power walked under the oak trees – or rather, Wendy power walked, I trotted alongside trying to keep up. "I don't know what to do next."

"Why does that sound so familiar? Oh, that's right, I've heard you say it before. Once. Or twice. Or was it 1200 times?"

"Well, this time I really don't." I pouted, sulking, considering whether to throw a full blown tantrum.

"Yes. You do. You always know what you want. You just won't admit it to yourself."

"I've lost my nerve. I thought it was bad making calls when nobody knew who I was, but now . . . I just can't do it."

"Let's get back to the subject. What do you want? Think now!" We crossed the road at the Girls' High School corner into the main part of the park, walking the path through the golf course. I squinted into the glare of the winter sun. "Are you thinking?"

"Yes, give me a minute."

"Just say the first thing that comes to mind."

"Well, I want some bigger projects. I loved doing the regular interviews for the book."

"Go on . . ."

"And I'd like to see where the recipe audios can go, I sense there are lots of possibilities there I haven't thought of yet. I want to do some more work with old clients, it's so much easier than facing new people all the time."

"But you can do that. You're good at it."

"Yeah, but it takes a lot of energy for me. I'm better with people I already know."

"Okay. What else?"

"I think that's enough, for now. If I could do those three things, that would keep me going."

"There! That wasn't so hard, was it? So what's the first thing?"

"Do the proposal."

"And call your old clients asking if they want to do anything else. Tell them about the book service, and the series of CDs like you're doing with me."

"What series of CDs? When?"

"I'd like to start this week. When are you free?"

53

Things were quiet around the house. Kate and Bernard had taken off for a week in the Marlborough Sounds so rehearsals were suspended. Steven was home and happy, working on the band's website, putting in an e-commerce section so he could sell their album on-line. The possibility seemed unlikely but it kept him happy. We took turns to walk the girls to and from school, sometimes both going down together. I decided to postpone my appointments till next week when I'd have the house to myself again. That gave me the chance to make the calls Wendy and I had talked about.

It felt weird at the start, I've never phoned a past client looking for new work before, but they were all happy to hear from me and a few asked to get together to discuss what we could do on a larger scale.

I was making lunch for Steven and myself on the Thursday when my mobile beeped. A text from Kate. I wiped my hands and picked up the phone. "Don't freak out. Girls on YouTube. Search Lilac."

I was more curious than concerned. What could it be?

"Steven?"

He called back from the conservatory. "Yeah?"

"Have you got a browser open?" I walked in and put my hand on the back of his chair.

"Just a sec." He saved and closed what he was doing and clicked on the Internet button. "What is it?"

"Kate said the girls are on YouTube."

"What? How?"

"From the concert, I guess. Was anyone filming?"

"Yeah, they were making one of those behind-the-scenes DVDs."

"Well, I guess that's what it is."

He found it quickly. "That can't be it, it has 10,000 views."

"It's them, look."

He pressed play, and there they were, my beautiful girls. At first it was just day clothes.

"Is it at the rehearsal?"

"Bernard had them sing for Lilac, so she could see if she wanted them to go on."

"Well, thank God they're dressed." I relaxed too soon. After a minute the clip started alternating between the daytime, jeans and t-shirt performance to the night time ritz and glitter and – oh my! I hadn't realised how much makeup they were wearing. It was the weirdest feeling, watching my seven year old, my nine year old, my 12 year old, dance like grownup pop stars. In the day shots they looked like children, but not in the rest. At the same time I was caught up in the energy of it. I've always loved this song, the attitude in it, and they do it so fantastically well. I put my arm around Steven's shoulder and pulled him close. "Oh my! What am I seeing?"

The clip finished and we stayed there, frozen, looking at the still image on the screen. After a minute I turned and leaned against the desk. "What do we do?"

"About what?"

"Do we get it taken off? What?"

"We probably could. Do you want to?"

"I don't know. How did they get it?"

"I'll make a couple of calls and find out. I think we wait for a bit to decide what to do."

"Yeah, okay." I walked like a zombie back to the kitchen and finished preparing lunch on auto pilot. Before ten minutes had passed I was back in front of the screen watching it again.

Steven came in with the phone in his hand. "The tour manager has already seen it. He said the camera operator edited this together just for fun, sent it to his girlfriend. She sent it on to a couple of friends. Who knows after that? We can definitely pull it if we want to. He's going to check with Lilac when it's day time in the States."

I nodded, eyes shifting back to the screen, transfixed.

"I think we leave it," he went on. "No-one knows who they are. Look, it's already at 11,000 views."

I looked at the number again. 1,000 views in the last 15 minutes. What was happening?

By the time the girls got home it was at 17,000 views. They were delighted, Greta especially.

"I told at News about being in the concert and Mrs Walsh told me off for lying. This will show her!"

"Why didn't you say something?"

"Oh, she's just an old witch, I'm used to her."

"Honey!" But she was too busy watching herself to listen to me.

"Look, look at us! We look really cool!"

Erica was running through to call her friends. "Look on YouTube! It's me!"

Late that night, after the girls had gone to sleep at long last, Lilac herself phoned.

"Hey, listen, I'm real sorry about this, that film was supposed to be secure until we edited the DVD. What do you want to do?"

My hand was shaking. Steven had the other phone. We looked at each other.

"Hi Lilac, Steven here. It's great of you to call."

"Do you want it off?"

Steven tilted his head at me. I glanced towards the girls bedroom and gave a tiny shake of the head.

"No, thanks, Lilac. If you're okay with it. The girls are so excited. They'd be devastated if it went."

"Okay, if you're sure. I'm mortified. It shouldn't have happened at all."

"Well, no problem, thanks again for calling, and for the money, too, the girls sent cards, did you get them?"

"Probably caught up in the fan mail. I'll ask my assistant to have a look. Those kids really are great. Any recording offers yet?"

"For Café Storm?"

"For the girls."

"Ah, no?"

"Well, okay, gotta run. Call me if you need anything."

Bernard came back from holiday effervescing. Kate looked for my reaction before breaking into her widest smile. "Did you see? 800,000 views this morning!"

"I've written some songs while I was away."

"For the band?"

"For the girls." Why did that last question and answer sound so familiar?

"Why?"

"Are you crazy? They're going to be the hottest thing in the country." He noticed my scowl. "Suitable songs, Tasha, with sweet little girl lyrics. Come on, you're not going to try to stop this!"

He sat down at the piano and started on a soft ballad-like tune. At the sound, Erica and Greta came running through. "Uncle Bernard!"

He winked at them. "Shh, listen to this."

The second time through the chorus they started joining in, catching the hook line, chiming sweetly. Charlotte appeared in the doorway pulling her new iPod out of her ears.

"Why didn't someone call me?"

She stood with the others, gathered around Bernard, watching his face as he sang.

"What do you think?"

"Really cool."

"Did you write that, Uncle Bernard?"

"I wrote it for you. How would you like to make an album?"

"Bernard . . ."

Kate stopped me and pulled me aside. "Just take a moment, Tasha, think before you react. I had a call from a record company this morning."

"Why . . ?"

"Because I'm Café Storm's manager. They want to sign the girls."

"But . . ."

"Just stay calm. You don't have to do anything this minute. Just think. This is a one in a million chance. If you can just let it roll."

Steven said to wait, give it a couple of days, we didn't need to decide anything yet.

"But Mum, we want to! It's the best thing ever!"

Erica was delighted, but I noticed Charlotte hanging back. "What is it, Hon?"

"I'm not sure."

"You feeling a bit shy?"

"I guess. Some of the girls . . ."

"What, Hon?"

"They said I'm 'full of myself'. They said just cause I'm on YouTube doesn't mean I'm anything special."

I wanted to slap someone.

"Course you're special! Don't you know they're jealous," Erica snorted.

Charlotte looked at me, questioning.

"Erica's right, Honey. That's all it is."

"Well, I don't like it, it was better when they just ignored me. And it's not just the mean girls. Margaret said she's not my friend any more. She said she's not famous enough for me."

"Charlotte . . ." What could I say? My concern for her was disappearing under my anger.

"Charlotte, are you going to give up every time someone doesn't like what you're doing?" Erica stood directly in front of her and stared into her eyes.

Charlotte's gaze flickered from Erica to me and back again.

"I want to do it. I want to make a record and be famous and no-one is going to stop me."

"Erica . . ."

"No, Mummy, no-one. And that includes you."

Okay. I was out of my depth. I handed the negotiations over to Kate and Steven. "I just want approval of schedules and costumes."

Kate looked at Steven. "All right." Her voice was cautious. "There were calls from two more recording companies today. I need some more guidance on this. I'm calling in Matt Plymouth, he's an agent in Auckland, he represents some of the biggest bands. He'll take 15% but he'll cut a better deal. I'll tell him what you said. Okay?"

"Okay."

The whole situation was too intense for me. I buried myself in my office, mechanically doing what I had to do for my business. Financially I had a feeling it wasn't going to be relevant for too much longer. The girls' money we would put aside, but Kate was working on a contract for the whole band, Steven, Bernard and Scott as well as Charlotte, Erica and Greta, and her as manager. "That gives us way more control over what happens." I would be the only one left out of the waterfall of cash. Never mind. I'd just have to get over it, get used to going along for the ride.

In the context of everything else, the acceptance of my Anthea proposal seemed pitifully minor, as did Wendy's 12 CD contract and two book/interview deals, one with a media expert and one with an organisational psychologist. The projects kept me busy, however, and I was grateful. There was too much happening that was outside my control. It would have driven me crazy if not for my headphones and my editing work.

The Anthea audio recipe book was a first trial of the concept, but one of the publishing company's editors saw the vision of it immediately. "Do this one as fast as you can, we'll get it out and buy shop front display space for it. If it takes off at all, we'll do our other four bestsellers straight away."

54

"Ms Stuart, I'm sorry to have to call you in again, but our little problem with Greta is escalating."

If Mrs Walsh was waiting for some sort of horrified response from me she was disappointed. I watched Greta, steely and defiant.

"She has become very popular within the class, but I'm sorry to say she remains unacceptably selective in her choice of playmates. I wonder what you propose we do about it."

"Mrs Walsh, once again, I don't see there is a problem. Greta, do you?"

"No. I just like playing with Jessica and Sam. Those other girls play silly games. I don't want to join in."

"Now, Greta! Ms Stuart, the girls have invented a perfectly charming game called Dance Video. They want Greta to play with them, and she persistently refuses."

"They can't dance, they're hopeless. I don't want to play." Greta turned to face me directly. "Mum, we play hideouts. There's only room for three and that Victoria is always trying to squeeze in. Then she says we have to play Dance Video but they're just copying and they're all stupid dancers. It's embarrassing."

"Greta!" Mrs Walsh was gearing up for a tirade. I stopped her.

"Perhaps we can leave this discussion for another time. I was going to send the letter in tomorrow, Greta will be out of school from the end of next week. She has a recording contract in the U.K. starting at the beginning of July, with two weeks of full time rehearsals beforehand. So if you can just keep things smooth for the next six days, perhaps all this will have blown over by the time she gets back."

I took Greta's hand and we left the classroom with the old trout gaping behind us. Truthfully I was grateful to get out of there without an irresponsible mother lecture. I was prepared for it, but all the same it was nicer without.

As we neared the school gate, where Charlotte and Erica were playing on the bars, I stopped and squatted down next to Greta. "Tell me, though, Hon, were you a bit unkind to the other girls? Did you tell them they were stupid?"

She looked at the concrete. "Yes."

"And what do you think of that?"

"Not very nice."

"You know what it's called? It's called arrogance, and people don't like it. It's one thing not to play with them, that's your choice. But if you're mean to them, you have to realise they may not play with you later if you want to."

"But they . . ."

"I'm not saying what you have to do or not do. I'm just letting you know."

She looked up at me with tears in her eyes. "Okay, Mummy."

"Okay." I hugged her. "Just one more week and then stardom awaits!"

Life had take on a hive-like buzz. We were used to regular rehearsals but never with such a focused purpose, and never involving the girls at a professional level. Every day after school, and then for the two following weeks they were at the café practising hard. Bernard was tearing his hair out finishing the two final songs, unused to creating under pressure.

"I don't think I can do it!" he wailed to the room in general one night when we were throwing together a late dinner before putting the girls to bed. There was something sweet and pitiable about him without his usual swaggering veneer.

"Here, sit down, drink this." I put a bottle of beer in front of him on the kitchen table, and patted his arm. He looked up at me. "You'll be fine, you're a genius."

"Really? Thanks, Tasha, that means a lot." A moment later he groaned and put his head on his arm, right hand still instinctively clutching his beer. "God, I really don't think I can do this."

"What's the big deal? You still have a week, I've seen you write a whole song in an evening."

His head came up just enough to look at me. "It doesn't happen on demand, though! Nothing's coming, I'm dry."

"You need to relax. Trust. Take some time out."

"Yeah right!" I thought more was coming in the same sceptical vein but his expression fell back into despondency. "It's not just that though. It's the whole thing. Abbey Road. It's a lifetime ambition that I thought I'd never get near, and - God! I'm not up to it, I'm not good enough."

I sat down on the chair next to his, put my hand on his and kissed his forehead. Once I had his full attention I looked seriously into his eyes. "Yes. You are." He gazed back at me, reading my sincerity. I had never noticed how clear his eyes were. I guess I usually avoided them. After a minute he sat up straight, squared his shoulders, took a deep breath.

"Okay."

Kate was running around organising clothes for the girls.

"It's a recording, they won't need them."

"It will help them get in the mood for performing if they dress right. And who knows what will happen while we're there? It's best to be prepared."

I had right of veto over the styles – Kate chose striking fabrics and we had them made up into streamlined but complete shapes. They had new jeans and ¾ white pedal pushers, the impact was in the tops, sparkling pinks and blues and oranges, some of them in simple t-shirt shapes, or tank tops, the wow coming from the light off the colours. She found hats, too, caps and trilbies which they wore slanted over one eye. Erica danced around the house in them at every spare moment, more dramatic than ever now she was going to be a star.

"This is what I've wished for my whole life! Stage, screen, glamour!"

"Come on, Erica, make up for performance only. It's time for bed."

She spun around theatrically. "As if I could ever sleep!" She held a wrist to her brow and fell backwards into the hallway. Kate laughed and put her arm across my shoulders.

"At least someone's remembering to enjoy herself." She indicated Charlotte with a tilt of the head, sitting very quiet on the sofa.

I nodded; Kate walked through to the kitchen. I sat down next to Charlotte.

"How are you, Darling?"

She looked up. "Just a little tired."

"Working too hard?"

"No. But I'm a little . . ."

I waited, head tilted.

"I'm a little nervous. I don't know what it's going to be like."

"You were at the recording studio with Café Storm. It'll be just like that."

"I guess. But what if I make a mistake? What if I make lots of mistakes?"

"Well, you probably will make some mistakes. So did Dad and Bernard and Scott. So? What did they do?"

"They laughed and did it again."

"Well!"

"But it's different this time, Mum, it feels different. Uncle Bernard is worried and Dad is distracted. I think this time is somehow different."

For a split second I considered lying to her, giving her cheery, empty encouragement. But that wasn't going to work. "Look, you know when you watched Lilac on stage?"

"Yeah."

"Did she look like she was having fun?"

Charlotte grinned. "Yeah, course."

"And was every note perfect? Were there no mistakes?"

"I don't know, I didn't notice."

"So what was more important, that she was perfect or that she was having fun? What made the biggest difference to the audience?"

Realisation spread across Charlotte's face. "They wanted to see her having fun."

"That's right. So what do you have to do in the studio?"

"Have fun?"

"Right. So practice this. I order you to have fun, right now." I put on a very non-p.c. German accent and put my finger across under my nose to represent a moustache.

Charlotte laughed "Mum! You can't order someone to have fun."

"Oh, so you're not giggling yourself silly?" I tickled her.

She writhed under my hands.

"So I'll stand outside the booth through the window, and whenever you are looking too serious, I'll do this moustache thing and you'll remember."

"Okay."

"You know what else?"

"What?"

"Having fun is contagious. When the others see you doing it, they'll catch it, too. Do you think that would help them?"

"Yeah, I think it would."

It seemed like only hours later we were on the plane and going. As we sat back into our seats, really on our way, the tension lifted.

Scott had brought Maria. I was relieved; I had sensed some dissatisfaction, heard him express wry ill-humour that if this was his big break it wasn't quite what he had expected.

He seemed okay now though, holding Maria's hand and smiling to himself. Maria opened her handbag and passed little activity packs to Greta, Erica and Charlotte.

"I thought you might not have had time to pack them."

She leaned back into her seat and Scott turned and kissed her. "Here we go." Bernard whistled a short section of a victory march and the rest of us laughed.

London was noisy and busy and overwhelming. Our hotel room overlooked a busy street and even with the window closed it was hard to get any real rest. Steven and I had a suite with the girls on rollaway beds in the living space. We wanted to have them near, in case they woke in the night and wanted us. At four the first morning I woke disoriented, jet lagged and with no hope of sleep returning. I went and sat in the weird summer light watching my daughters sleep. I wanted coffee but it was too early, I didn't want to wake them as I snuck out.

By 5:30 we were all up and wondering what we could do. We dressed and hit the streets, deciding it was too much of a cop out to eat at the 24 hour McDonalds down the road. We found a big hotel with breakfast starting at 6. The buffet was perfect, quiet at that time of day. I sat back and inhaled the opulence, gilt and chandeliers and heavy linen napkins. I could live like this every day. Greta and Erica came back full of the wonders of the buffet, putting their plates on the table and going straight back for more. Steven was foraging contentedly. Charlotte waited for me.

"Okay."

With our folder of tickets and hotel vouchers the recording company had sent a beautiful wad of £20 notes "for incidental expenses during your stay." Steven and I had looked at each other and laughed. This was the moment we realised that things had really changed.

Breakfast for the five of us was £75, $200! Outrageous, but so, so worth it.

We had a couple of days to recover from jet lag before the studio was booked. Our company contact had left a message at the hotel offering to book shows or suggest sightseeing, whatever we wanted.

The hotel was just across the road from the big Kensington museums. We spent the first morning at the Natural History Museum – Greta has a mania for dinosaurs – then Charlotte and I strolled through the Victoria and Albert while Steven took Greta and Erica back to the hotel to rest.

Charlotte seemed deep in thought.

"You're quiet. Are you okay?"

She turned to me with a peaceful smile and nodded. "Yeah, I'm fine."

55

Our various groups went separate ways during our free days, only coming together again when two black cabs pulled up on the Thursday morning to take us to Abbey Road.

Bernard's face was red and shining. Kate seemed more impatient than normal, snapping at his excited antics.

"What's up with you?" I whispered when we were in the cab. She had engineered to be separate from Bernard.

"It's being back in this country, it's driving me mad. I can't talk about it now."

We had a tour of the studio, catching sight of a couple of rock legends and some other groups like us who were star-struck. We met the record company representative, the producer and the sound engineers.

The plan had been to try recording the whole band at once, on the basis that that was what the girls were used to, so it might go smoother that way. Once Greta had messed up the first four takes, however, and without being aware at all until Erica let fly at her, they decided to lay down the guys tracks first and bring the girls in to do the vocals, hopefully that afternoon.

The company rep mistook Kate for me and asked if the girls would like to go for hot chocolate. She was clearly confused and embarrassed when Kate deferred to me.

"I'm so sorry, you . . ."

"Yeah, I know, we look so much alike. I'm their aunt, I manage the band. It's a long story. Anyway, Tasha?"

We went to a café just around the corner, leaving Kate in the booth with the guys. I felt a twinge of jealousy at missing the recording experience to play mother, but I would get to watch later when the girls were in the booth. Carline took us shopping, in a black cab back to Harrods where Greta and Erica went mad in the toy department. Charlotte found her way to the books and was still sitting reading when Carline got the message for us to head back.

"Erica and Greta have a teddy bear each – do you want one, too, or a book?" Charlotte looked up with surprise, as if she had totally forgotten where she was. "Book then?" And I lead her to the counter.

We found Scott, Steven and Bernard elated, things had gone really well since we left. We took Greta through the introduction exactly as they had recorded it and Bernard sang her through it a couple of times till she got it. I stood behind the glass and gave my moustache signal to Charlotte. She burst out laughing. The others turned to look at her, then grinned, too. She gave me the thumbs up.

Five times through and lots of mistakes. Greta was upset by Erica's eye rolls and Charlotte withdrew into herself as the tension built. There was a hushed discussion in the level room about whether they could record each voice separately. Steven stepped in. "No, the sound is about the energy of the three of them together."

"But they've got to be having fun." It was the first time I had put an opinion into the discussion, and everyone turned to stare. I appealed to Bernard. "They've got to be having fun, I'm right aren't I? That's what's wrong here."

Bernard nodded. "Yeah, Tash, that's it. So what can we do?"

"Bern, right from the start, when you first started teaching them the songs, how did you do it? They loved it right from the start."

"Well, I sort of hammed it up, fading back once they started to get it."

"Okay, so how can you do that now?"

He considered for a moment. "Okay, I think I've got it."

He went into the recording booth and started flapping his arms. We all listened through the speakers.

"Okay, guys, it's time to stop having so much fun. This is a serious business."

Greta giggled. I knew he had her.

"And Erica, I want you to stop being so nice to your sister, it's making her too happy, all right" Erica nodded, smiling. "Charlotte, you're doing okay, but please tone down that grin, it's scaring the natives."

They were all laughing now.

"Now I'm going back out there, through that glass, and I'm going to behave with absolute decorum, show you how it's supposed to be done, and you follow my lead."

They nodded, exchanging glances, and watched him out of the room with curiosity.

"Okay, clear the way," Bernard muttered as he came back into the engineering booth. He pushed in chairs, waved Steven and me back so there was a corridor of space. He pressed the button so they could hear him. "Are you ready? Then let's go."

And as the music began to play he started doing a sort of wild bird dance up and down the room, flapping his arms and lifting his knees and mouthing the words of the song. Seriously, it sounds stupid, but it was one of the funniest things I've ever seen. The girls' eyes opened wide and they started to laugh. They were late with their entrance but by the middle of the song they were in full enthusiastic swing.

They finished and Bernard pushed the button again. "And once more" he panted. This time they did it. As they grinned and smiled their way through a perfect take Bernard slowed and finally stopped. The last chord faded out and we all started cheering. The sound engineer flicked the switch so they could hear us. They had been grinning at each other but at the sound they turned to the glass and beamed. Erica lead them in a bow.

"That was great. Same time tomorrow for track number two."

56

About day three of recording I was getting anxious for news from home. Anthea's audio recipe book was going on sale this week. The company had invested in feature stands for the large book shops – the book would be displayed along with the CD. If there was a reasonable response to this then there would be a television advertisement, a big splash of marketing. The displays had gone up the day we left. I was sorry not to be there to see them. I knew it was very early, but by now they would have the first week's estimated figures and I was on tenterhooks to hear how it had gone.

I telephoned Anthea.

"Have patience," she said, not sounding patient at all herself. "It's too soon to know."

"But you must have some kind of feel for it."

"Well, I did go in and take a peek one afternoon," she admitted. "People were looking. Someone even picked one up, looked at it curiously. But then they shrugged and put it back. So I took some over to the main recipe book section, I figured people there are serious buyers. And I did see one sell from there. It's a new thing; it's going to take a while." Her voice on this last sentence echoed my frustration.

"So they won't do the ad?"

"At this point probably not." I could hear her shrug.

"Damn."

We finished the call on this unsatisfactory note. It was the next day in the recording studio that I had my flash of brilliance.

"Anthea?"

"Tasha? What time do you call this?"

"I'm sorry, I waited as long as I could. What about your email list?"

"My what?"

"Your email list. Did you let them know?"

"I don't know what the fuck you're talking about." Anthea isn't at her best first thing in the morning.

"Go get a cup of coffee. I'll wait."

I heard a sigh, a beep, a scrape of cup and saucer. 30 seconds later the characteristic click of a Nespresso pod and the buzz of the brewing coffee. A pause, a happier sigh.

"Okay, what?"

"Did you send out an email to your list announcing the audio book?"

"Wow. No, I didn't. I was so focused on the shops, the displays."

"Well, do it."

"Sure, I'll do it today."

Two days later I was back on the phone. "Anthea, did you know Julian Gull was on your email list?"

"Not until he phoned me to ask for your number. My God, Julian Gull! He's the god of celebrity chefs! What did he say?"

"He wants me to go there to record his last book. As soon as I can. I'm torn, I'd be there now but we have another week of recording."

"And they need you there?"

The sense of guilt was immediate as I considered her question. Technically they didn't, but was I really considering bailing on my husband and children in their hour of triumph?

"Well . . ."

"I don't know about you, but I wouldn't keep Julian Gull waiting for anything. What if he decides to use someone else?"

I felt sick as I hung up the phone. I knew what I wanted to do. But surely I couldn't. The album was progressing well but each day it got harder to rev up the enthusiasm. Just the day before I'd had to call a halt with Greta in tears.

"She's seven years old, for goodness sake. If she needs to rest she should rest."

That had put them behind schedule, and I was Cruella de Ville, the producer whispering to Kate behind my back. I didn't hear Kate's answer but she looked guilty when she turned to see me so near. She was showing the strain more than anyone.

That afternoon Kate disappeared completely, returning only after dinner that evening. Bernard ate with us, face long.

We all went to bed early. I closed the door of the bedroom and followed Steven to the bathroom as he went to clean his teeth. Not catching his eye in the mirror I began speaking before I had even consciously decided what to say. "Do you think you could all do without me for a couple of days?"

He turned. "What? Why?"

"That offer from Julian Gull. I want to do it."

"Sure, but now? Why does it need to be now?"

"This is a big chance for me, and I'm no use here, I'm just the dragon everybody tries to avoid." As I said it I knew it was true. This wasn't just about wanting to take this chance. I resented having to be the grownup, manage everybody's egos. I had been pepping up Bernard, jollying and defending the girls. Steven didn't ask for much but he was very self-contained, looking after himself and not noticing too much what was going on around him. And something else which distracted me for a moment. "And what's up with Scott, anyway? He looks like someone peed in his shoes."

"No-one thinks you're a dragon. We need you here. I need you here. I know it seems long and hard but I'm loving it, really. I want you here."

I pouted. Although it was kind of nice to hear him say it.

"Oh, and Scott, he's having a little tantrum about artistic purity. Says he didn't sign up to be some wimp in a teeny-bopper backup band. Maria's gaga over Greta, you know that, and she's started to give Scott the hard word about getting pregnant."

"I'd have thought he'd be delighted. He's been asking her to marry him for months."

"You wouldn't know it about him – he hides it well – but he really likes being the centre of attention. He's being a brat. Ignore him."

He put his toothbrush down and turned to me, wrapping his arms around me. I felt his guitarist's muscles through the silk of my nightgown. He did that eyebrow thing he does, a comic Don Juan. I glanced at the bedroom door. He bounded over, locked it and bounded back.

"Let me explain to you why you want to stay with me."

His crude Spanish accent made me laugh. He leaned down and picked me up, staggering the two steps to the bed.

"Women find the passion of the musician an irresistible aphrodisiac."

I stifled a laugh. I nodded with mock-seriousness, my hair rumpling on the pillow. "You're right, we do."

TASHA STUART INTERVIEWS . . .

57

Next morning I phoned Julian Gull and scheduled recording for the following Monday. Kate was distracted and terse when I told her.

"We're filming the video next week."

"You're what?"

"I told you, the video, for the "Break my heart" single. You knew we were discussing it."

"Yes, but I thought . . ."

"Look, we're here, and the video needs to be ready in case the single is a hit straight out of the box. Which it probably will be, we'll put a clip from the video on YouTube, you know what's likely to happen. We need it ready. So it's next week."

"Kate! Why didn't you tell me?"

"Why didn't you ask? If you took more interest instead of leaving everything to me."

The threat of having to postpone this opportunity, of maybe losing it, hijacked me.

"You're the big manager, I'm just the in-the-way mother, why should I expect to have any say."

Kate grabbed my arm and pulled me out of the booth into the corridor.

"For God's sake, Tasha, grow up. Don't throw that mother thing in my face, I've been working my tail off, and not for me."

"Not for you, right! You've been riding the band's coat tails to success for nearly a year, not for you! You'd be waiting tables if it wasn't for this."

"No, if it wasn't for me, someone else would be here. I taught them discipline and I got them their first breaks. They'd be begging pub gigs back home, or off the map completely. But don't worry, I won't be 'riding their coat tails' much longer, I've had enough."

"Likely! What else would you do after this?"

Kate slumped back against the wall. A passing musician stared at us.

"Kate?"

"Maybe what I wanted to do before but couldn't."

"What are you talking about?" A suspicion dawned. "Kate, where were you this morning? Bernard came down to breakfast like a bear with a sore head."

"Last night, I went up to Cambridge. I was with Daniel."

"And last Friday?"

"The same."

"And what happened?"

She looked at me, her face suddenly stricken. "Oh, God, Tasha! He's so good, so kind, he loves me so much."

"You're thinking of going back?"

"I'm thinking of going back."

"And Bernard?"

"Yeah. Bernard. I feel bad, I'll have to tell him. But Bernard's a kid, Daniel's a grownup. My mind's in a spin, I don't know what to do, there's too much happening. Maybe it's for the best, for everyone. Like you said, I've run my usefulness with the band, they need a professional. Bernard's a star now, he'll be fighting off offers, he'll be married within a year."

"And you? Are you sure you know what you want?"

"Me? Sure? When was I ever sure of anything?"

"Just always. You always know what to do."

She laughed. "I don't know where you get these crazy ideas. But you're right, this time. I know I love him."

Love. In all the years, with all her guys, I had never heard her use that word before. But even as I registered this, my mind was running forward. "Can I ask you a favour?"

"Sure, Kid, anything."

"Stay till the video's done. We can't actually do it without you."

"Yeah, you could. But I'll stay."

TASHA STUART INTERVIEWS . . .

58

It felt wrong, but I kept my appointment with Julian Gull, meeting him at his Lincolnshire estate the next Monday afternoon. It was Charlotte who was hardest to leave, heading for the film studio with her bag full of costumes. Her eyes pleaded with me to stay but she didn't say it out loud.

Steven did. "I wish you weren't going."

"I have to. This is really big for me."

"I know. Take care. We'll miss you."

Kate hissed and glared and said nothing.

I felt like me again. Not the spare wheel on an 18 wheel trailer, but like I meant something on my own. Julian was charming, funny, very welcoming. He had a neighbour with a soundproof room so we went there three hours each morning and afternoon and in three days the book was done. I downloaded the files to my computer, backed them up onto a CD which I gave to Julian. "Not to listen to, just a backup."

I talked to the girls every day. They were having fun, especially Erica, and maybe sounding a little full of themselves. "Mum, the director said I was born to be a star."

"It's so cool dancing in front of the cameras, that Victoria would spit if she could see me."

I didn't remind Greta that she probably would.

"Hi, Mum."

"Charlotte darling, sounds like you're doing great."

"Yeah, I like the dancing, but my legs are really tired. When are you coming back?"

"Well, I'm not sure. I thought tomorrow, but Julian has asked if we can record some more. You could come and see me when you're finished."

There was a silence. I bit my top lip, feeling horribly selfish. "When will you be finished filming?"

"I don't know. We did the whole song, and dancing, over and over again, but I heard the director saying something about the moor sections. I think we're going somewhere else tomorrow."

"Okay. Let me talk to Kate."

"Hey there. How's the famous interviewer?"

"Good. Listen, are you nearly finished? What's happening?"

"Well . . . the original plan was to do the whole thing in the studio, and then play around afterwards putting in different scenes – you know, cityscapes, wilderness, desert, moonscapes – but Vern, the director, thinks a real change of scene would work better, more in tune with the YouTube piece, with just two scenes, studio and somewhere wild. He thinks Yorkshire, high on the moors, so he can get sky silhouettes. He's got a location in mind, but we can wait till you get back. Are you coming tomorrow?"

"I was just telling Charlotte. Julian's asked if we can do another three books, right now. It would take maybe a week."

"And you want to."

"Yes."

"And you can't put it off."

"I don't want to. Everything's going so well, and I . . ."

"You don't need to say any more."

This made me feel guiltier than anything.

"So what's new? Everyone happy?" The false brightness in my voice didn't fool either of us.

"Bernard says he is in the depths of despair at the thought of leaving me. Scott has thrown his toys out of the cot and gone home – don't worry, we have enough footage for the video, that will be okay. Steven is missing you and keeps saying how much he supports your career. And me, well, don't you worry about me, in between pacifying Bernard, holding off Daniel, agreeing with Steven and pandering to your pop-star kids, there's not much to worry about."

"Kate . . ."

"Forget it. Do what you need to do."

59

We continued recording and in another two days we had all but finished the second book. In the evenings I did some editing and Julian was already playing with downloads from his website. "I've cleared it with the publisher, this is test marketing. Just to see if people will pay a few pence to download a dish or two."

It was exciting, and at the same time I felt absent, like I wasn't really here or anywhere else either. I hadn't been able to talk to the children the night before, they were out of coverage and I didn't know which hotel they were in.

Kate phoned the next night, sounding past her wits' end.

"Before you say anything, let me talk. I can't listen to your jolly crap any more. We're all in a mess. Greta tripped in a rabbit hole today and hurt her ankle, she screams if anyone touches it. I don't know how serious it is, whether she really shouldn't use it or whether she's just throwing a tantrum. She keeps asking for you. Erica's loving it, too much if you ask me, frankly I've had enough of her. I've sent her downstairs, wrapped in a fur stole, to prance in front of the hotel staff because any minute now I'll strangle her with it. And Charlotte, well, she just gets quieter and quieter. She's not dancing right. Nothing I say gets through and Steven doesn't seem to have a clue how to handle her. They're making her look like a woman, and I think it's freaking him out. The costumes are fine, but some of the moves – the director thought she was 15."

"She's 13, and her birthday was only last month!"

"I know that! I corrected him but he still seems to forget, and she's really uncomfortable, but she won't talk to me. I know you don't want to hear this, Tasha, but you need to come."

"Kate, I can't! You know what this means to me. Three more books! It's a dream come true for me, to work with someone like this."

"Tasha, I'll say this straight. Tell him to wait. You had something to prove and you proved it. You're just as big a success as they are, over there with your big famous chef. Now get your head out of your arse and come back and look after your children. They need you."

I didn't have a chance to answer. She was gone. I lay back on the pillows of my lemon-coloured floral-print bed and let my tears flow.

Since when had Kate been the voice of reason and conscience? I wanted to discount her words but they came back over and over. You had something to prove and you proved it. Was that all I was doing? In the end it didn't take long to see.

I found Julian leaning over a cookbook on the kitchen bench, flicking through the pages, making notes. "Hey, just getting ready for tomorrow. Something up?"

I took a big breath of air, summoning courage.

"Julian, would you mind if we delayed a couple of days?"

"Sure, no, why?"

"Can we use the Internet? I want to show you something."

Julian's quiet, thoughtful 14-year-old son came in while we were watching YouTube. "Hi Robert," Julian said. I turned and saw the boy's eyes wide.

"And these are your daughters? This is what you would have been doing this week? Why didn't you say?"

I shrugged, feeling silly. "We had an arrangement."

He looked at me closely. "We did, but . . ."

"Anyway, I'd like to go over to Yorkshire while they finish filming, it should only be a couple of days. We can continue next week. Is there somewhere I can hire a car to get there?"

"It would take you all day to drive. I'll call a helicopter, you'll get there in an hour. If you leave early you'll arrive before breakfast."

Julian helped me with my bag, walking with me across his wide lawn. "Ever been in a helicopter before?" he shouted over the noise of the rotor and engine. I nodded. If only he knew.

I turned and waved at him and Robert as they stood on the doorstep.

60

Five mouths fell open in the hotel restaurant as I walked with my windswept hair through the door. Bernard only stared morosely.

"Mummy, was that you in the helicopter?" Erica cried.

Kate smiled. "Hey, Kid, it's good to see you."

I kissed Steven and sat down between Greta and Charlotte, first checking with Greta before gently removing her foot from the chair. "Is it really hurt bad?" I whispered.

"Not really," she whispered back, looking up from under her lashes to see if she was in trouble.

I put my arm around Charlotte, who leaned gratefully into me.

"Now, what about breakfast? Those big famous chefs don't feed you very well."

As we left the restaurant I took Charlotte aside. "What's up, Honey?"

"I got my period. We're dancing and there aren't any toilets where we're filming, and I didn't want to ask to go in the car all the time, but . . ."

She looked over at the others. The driver was ready and everyone was waiting for us.

"Let them wait," I said. "We'll get you sorted."

I guided her to the ladies' and waited outside the cubicle. "We need a signal for when you want me to take you to a toilet. What will it be?"

"I could do The Eyebrow." We both laughed.

"Maybe something bigger, that I can see from a distance."

"Well, what if I just wave at you?"

"That'll be fine."

We walked out to the door arm-in-arm. Steven was looking at his watch. I saw Charlotte notice. She looked back at me. "What are you going to tell them?"

"Nothing. A lady never has to explain the time she takes getting ready."

We were all in exuberant spirits as we drove out to the film site. The director looked from Kate to me. "Ah, Mrs Wendel. This is good news!"

"Ms S . . . Just call me Tasha."

"Today we're looking for big smiles from Greta and Charlotte, and some big dancing. The wind is down today, so it should all be easy.

"Erica, share your fun with your sisters, smile at each other as well as the camera."

Lots of dancing, lots of fixing hair, four trips to the local pub bathroom, it was a good day's filming. Whenever Charlotte looked uncomfortable with a dance move, or I thought it too mature – the director was choreographing the girls slightly differently – I stepped over and firmly told him that we needed a change.

Dinner that night was an hilarious affair. It felt great to be part of the family again. The next day we were done.

61

The following morning we packed up ready to go. Steven and Bernard, Erica and Greta were heading back to London and home in a couple of days' time. Charlotte was staying on with me while I completed my recipe recordings. Julian said Robert was ecstatic, apparently very eager to meet her. Kate was going back to Cambridge.

We waved off the boys and younger girls as the car wound out of the circular driveway. I hadn't heard what Kate said to Bernard before he left, but I'd seen a lift of his eye, a flicker of gratitude, the beginning of optimism returning.

Steven and I kissed. "I'm really glad you came."

"Yeah, me, too, I can't believe I was going to miss it."

"See you in a few days."

"A week at the most. Take care of my girls for me."

I followed Kate back into the hotel. True to form she hadn't finished packing. She had an hour or two before her train. Our helicopter would be here any minute.

"Hey, Babe, time to say goodbye." I felt the prick of a tear.

"Yeah, Sis, I'll miss you."

"Are you sure you want to do this? We'll miss you at home, too."

"Nah, you don't need me anymore. I'll go where I'm wanted." There was an expression in her eye I hadn't seen there before: soft, vulnerable, maybe a little bit scared, a little hopeful.

"Say 'Hi' to Daniel for me. I'd like to meet him some day."

"He sort of knows you already."

"Really? How?"

"He asked me about you. I told him you're like me, only better."

~ ~ ~ ~ ~ ~ ~ ~ ~ ~ ~ ~ ~ ~ ~ ~

If you have enjoyed

Tasha Stuart interviews . . .

Please email jennifer@jennifermanson.co.nz
to join my mailing list and receive information
about further publications, or see
www.jennifermanson.co.nz.

I welcome your feedback.

Please post your review on Facebook.
Search for "Jennifer Manson Author"

With my very great thanks,

Jennifer.